NOODLEHEADS SEE THE FUTURE

by Tedd Arnold
Martha Hamilton
and Mitch Weiss

illustrated by Tedd Arnold

Holiday House / New York

Specially for Grace,
who can often see the future!

Text copyright © 2017 by Tedd Arnold, Martha Hamilton and Mitch Weiss
Illustrations copyright © 2017 by Tedd Arnold
All Rights Reserved
HOLIDAY HOUSE is registered in the U.S. Patent and Trademark Office.
Printed and Bound in November 2016 at Toppan Leefung, DongGuan City, China.
The artwork was rendered digitally using Photoshop software.
www.holidayhouse.com
First Edition
1 3 5 7 9 10 8 6 4 2

Library of Congress Cataloging-in-Publication Data

Names: Arnold, Tedd, author, illustrator. | Hamilton, Martha, author. |
Weiss, Mitch, 1951- author.
Title: Noodleheads see the future / by Tedd Arnold, Martha Hamilton and Mitch
Weiss ; illustrated by Tedd Arnold.
Description: First Edition. | New York : Holiday House, [2017] | Series:
Early chapter book | Summary: Inspired by folktales about fools from
around the world, brothers Mac and Mac Noodlehead exasperate Uncle Ziti,
are fooled by their friend Meatball, and make a garden for their mother.
Identifiers: LCCN 2016004460 | ISBN 9780823436736 (hardcover)
Subjects: | CYAC: Fools and jesters—Fiction. | Brothers—Fiction. | Humorous stories.
Classification: LCC PZ7.A7379 Nu 2017 | DDC [E]—dc23 LC record available at
https://lccn.loc.gov/2016004460

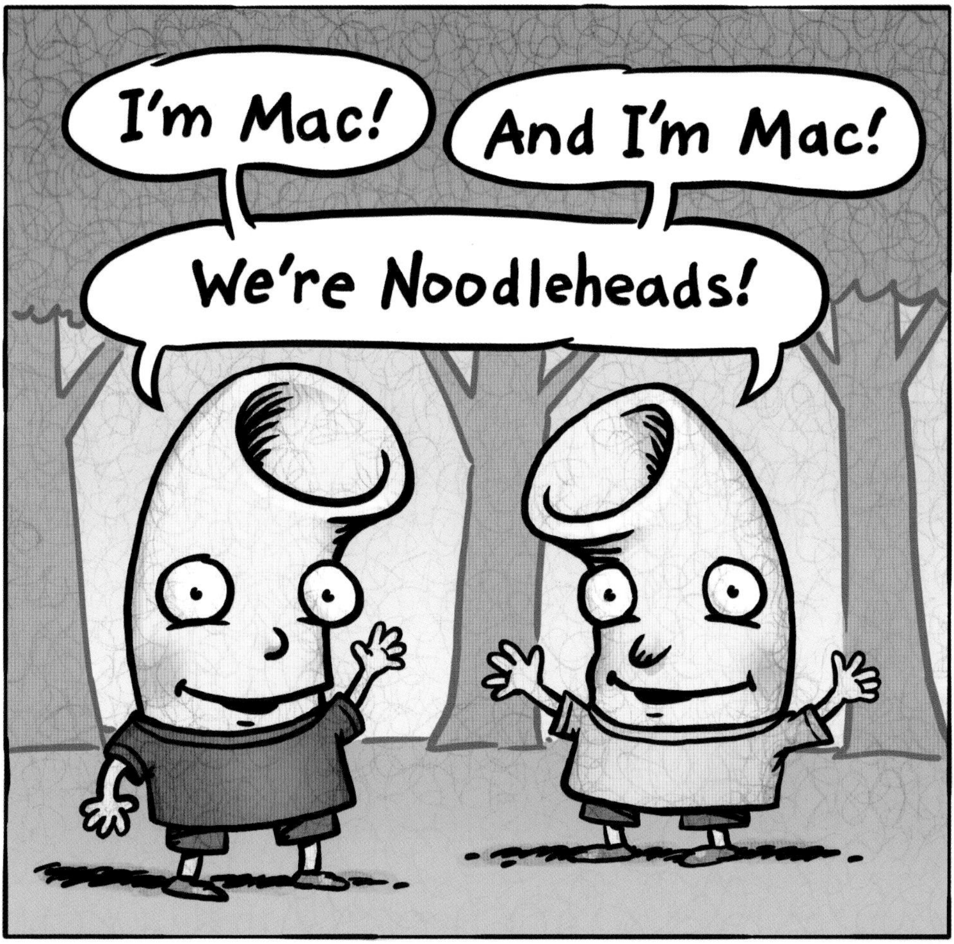
I'm Mac!
And I'm Mac!
We're Noodleheads!

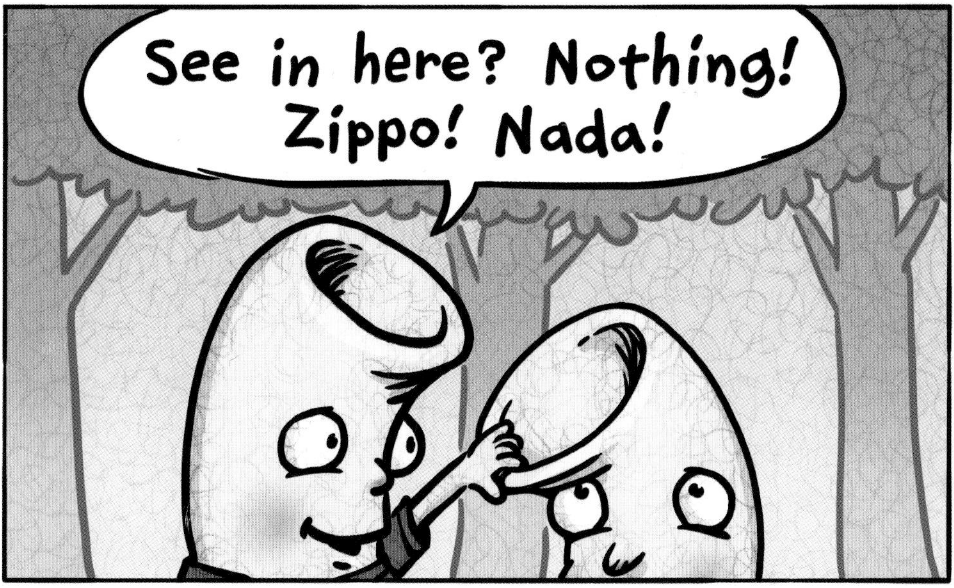
See in here? Nothing!
Zippo! Nada!

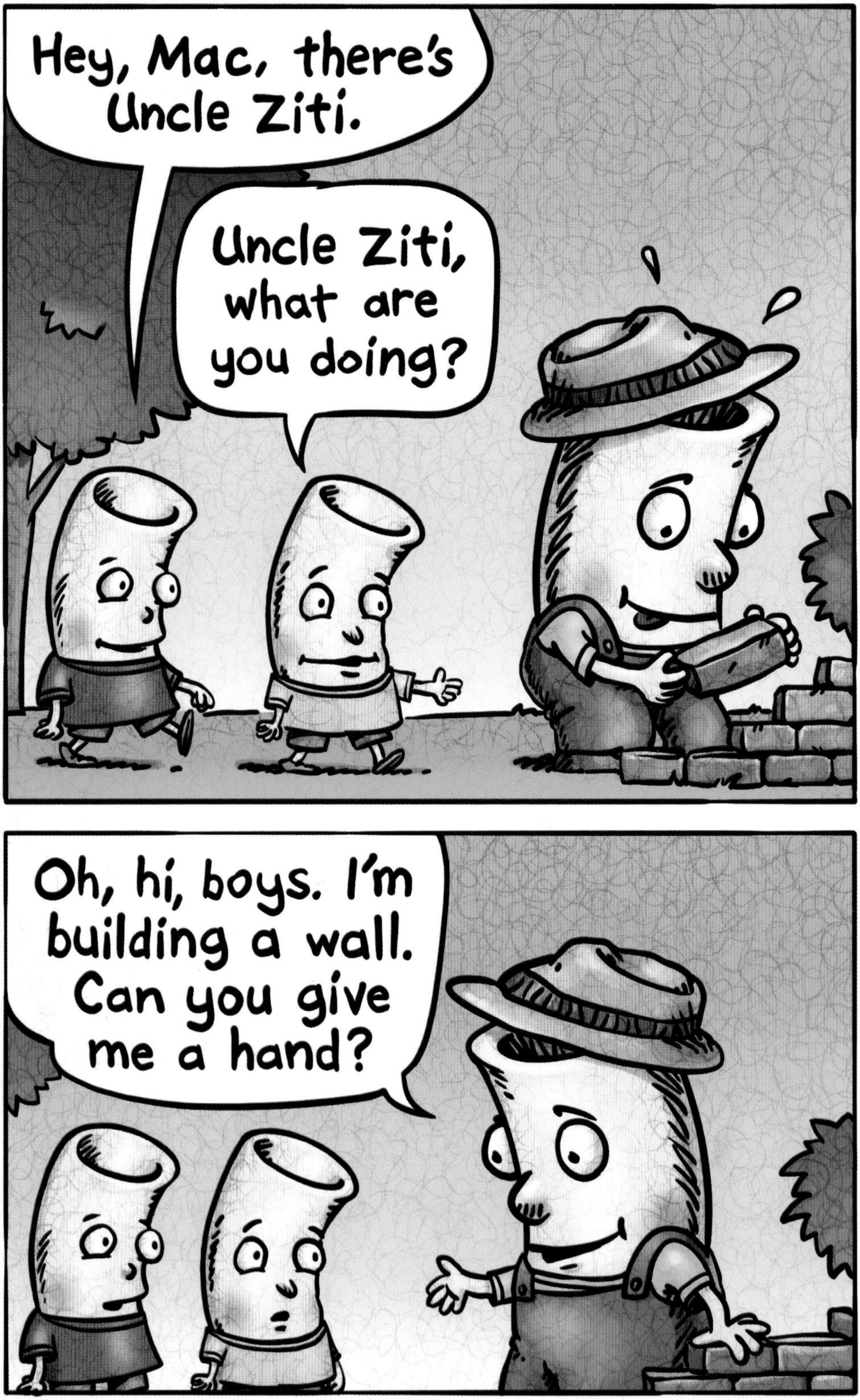
Hey, Mac, there's Uncle Ziti.
Uncle Ziti, what are you doing?
Oh, hi, boys. I'm building a wall. Can you give me a hand?

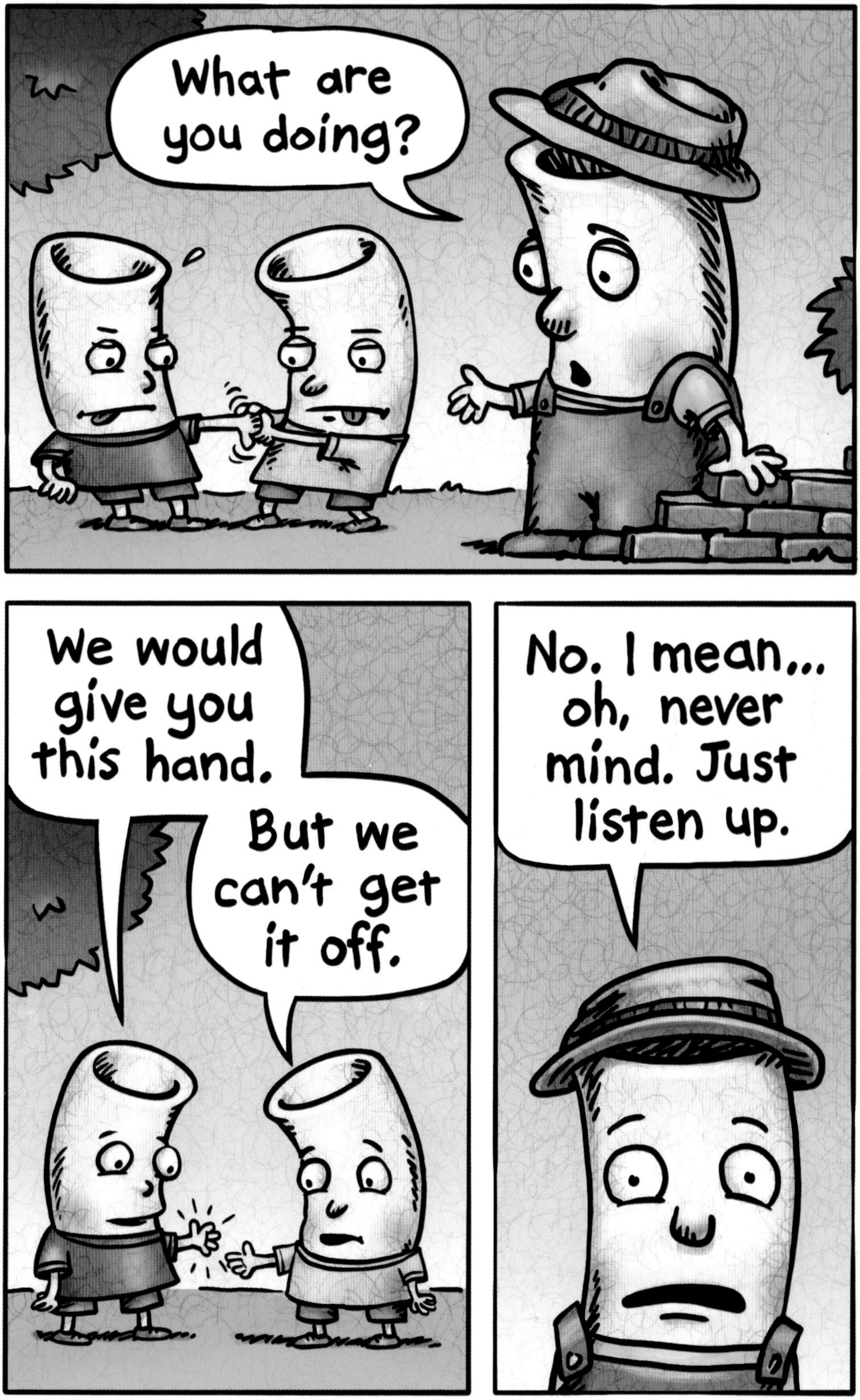
What are you doing?
We would give you this hand.
But we can't get it off.
No. I mean... oh, never mind. Just listen up.

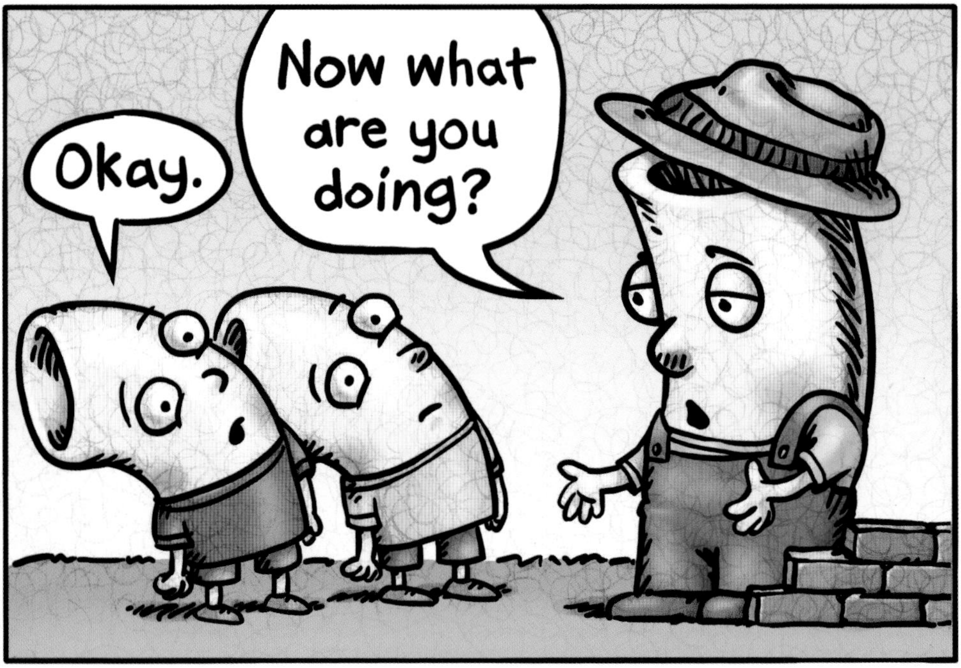
Okay.
Now what are you doing?

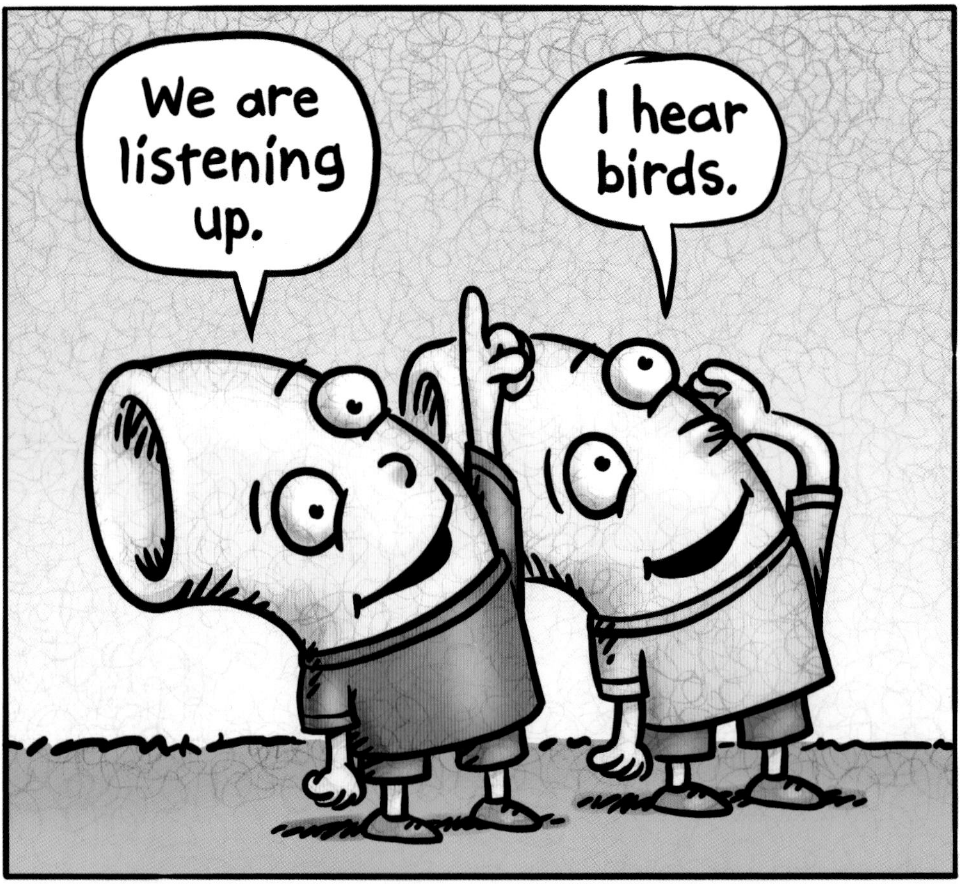
We are listening up.
I hear birds.

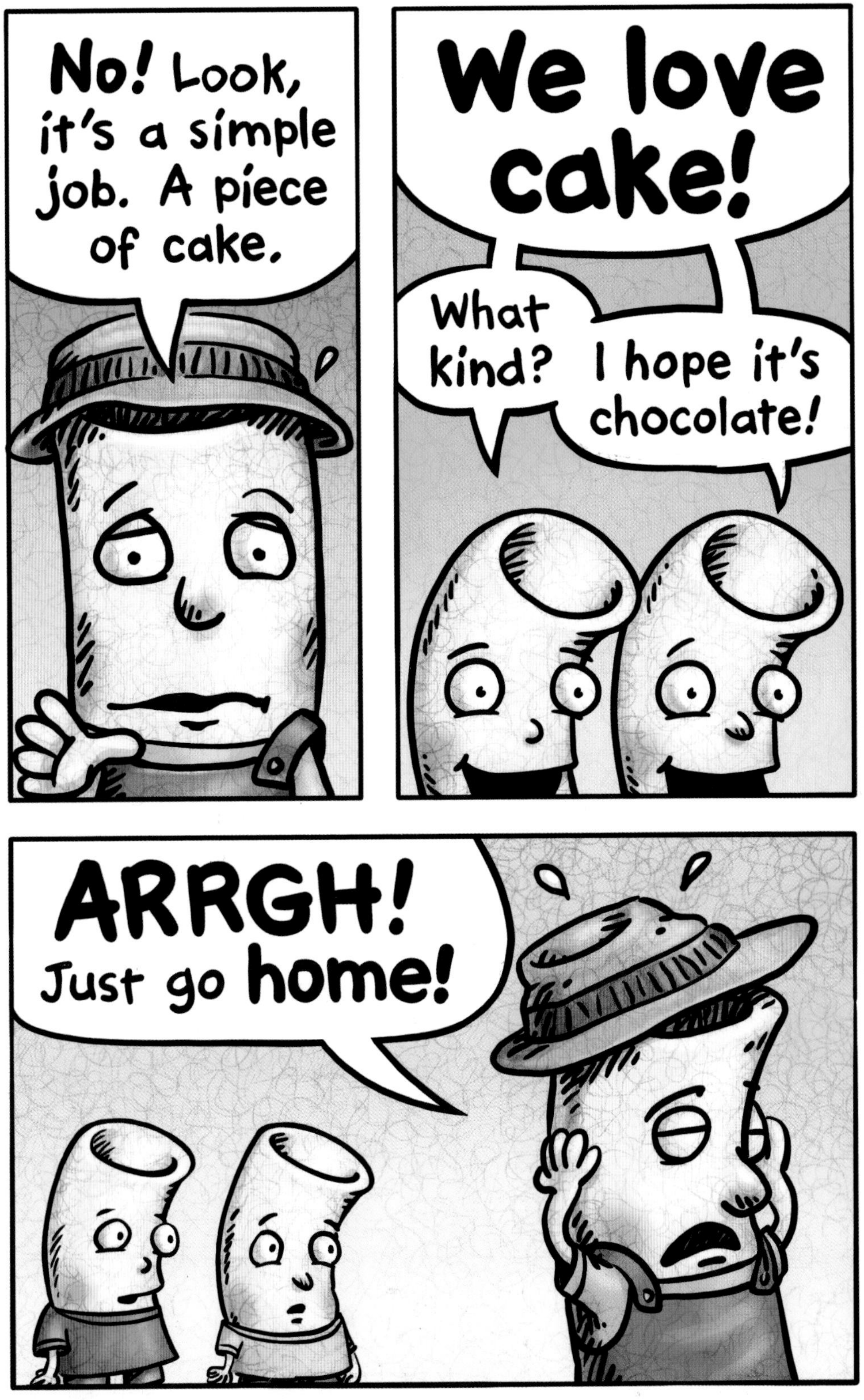
No! Look, it's a simple job. A piece of cake.
We love cake!
What kind?
I hope it's chocolate!
ARRGH! Just go home!

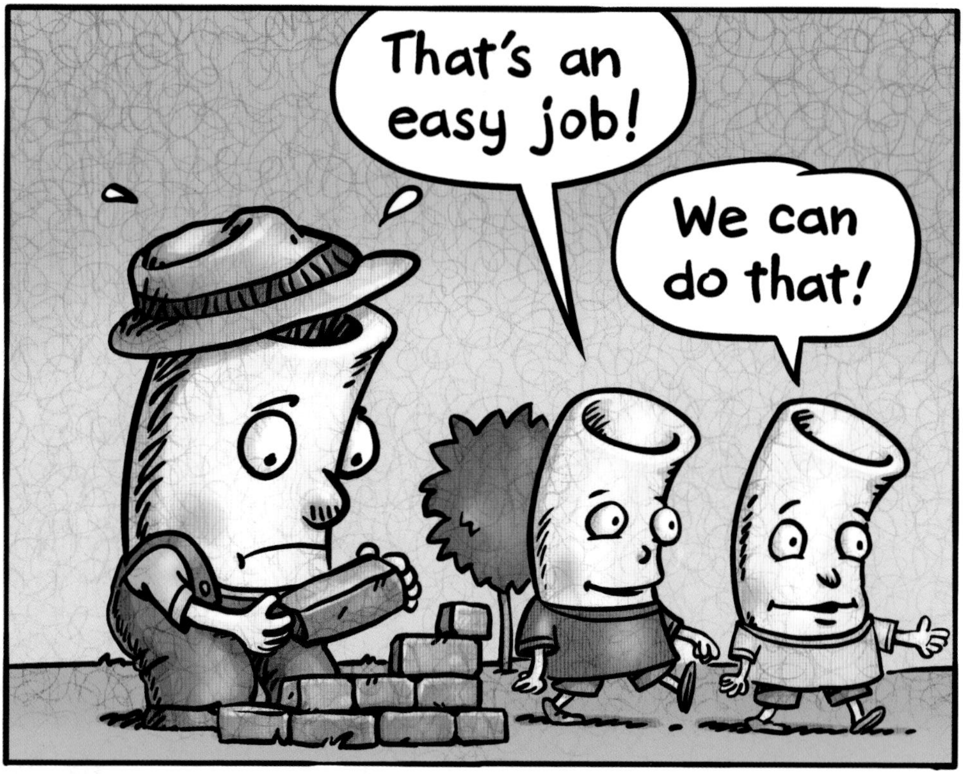
That's an easy job!
We can do that!

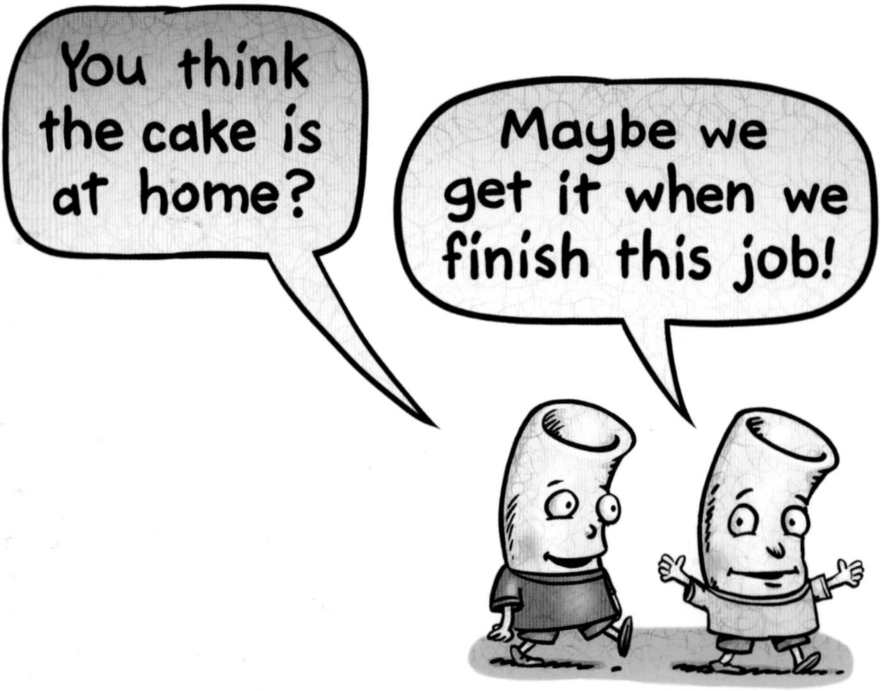
You think the cake is at home?
Maybe we get it when we finish this job!

NOODLEHEADS SEE THE FUTURE

CHAPTER 1

GETTING FIREWOOD

One day, Mac and Mac found their mother in the side yard.

What are you doing?

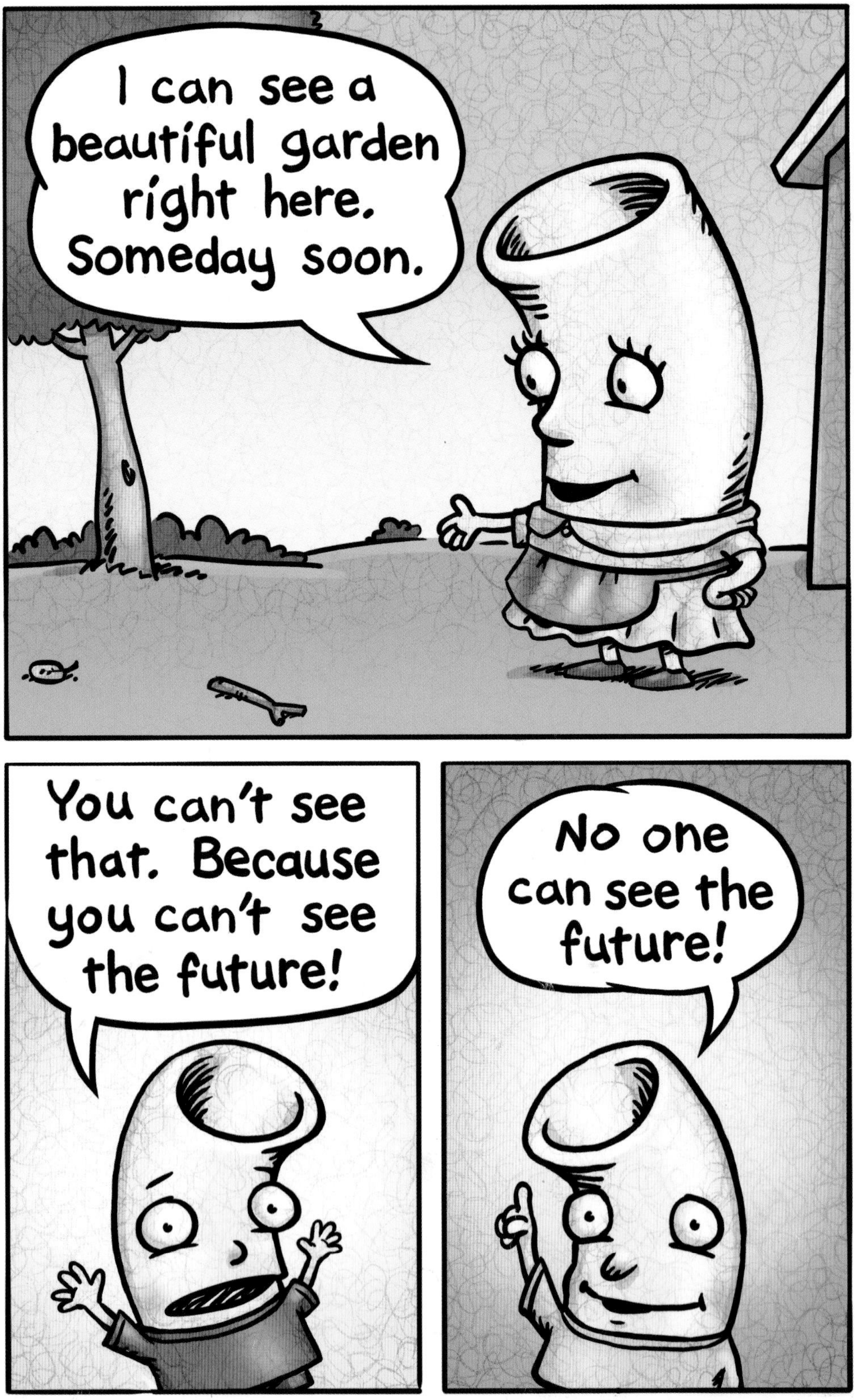
I can see a beautiful garden right here. Someday soon.
You can't see that. Because you can't see the future!
No one can see the future!

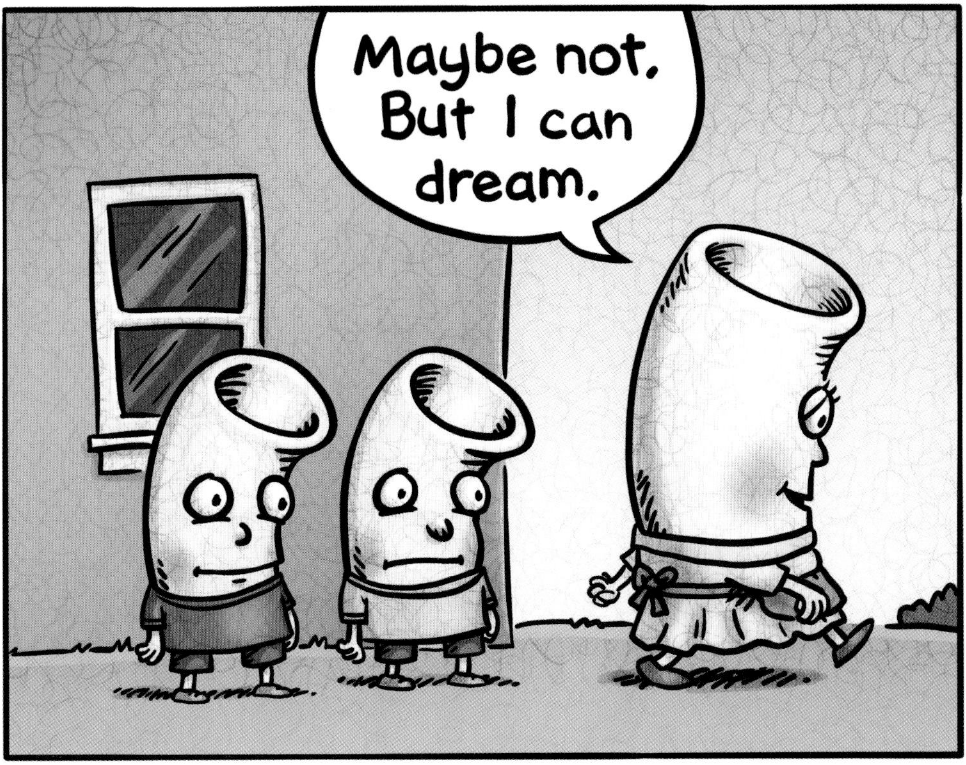
Maybe not. But I can dream.

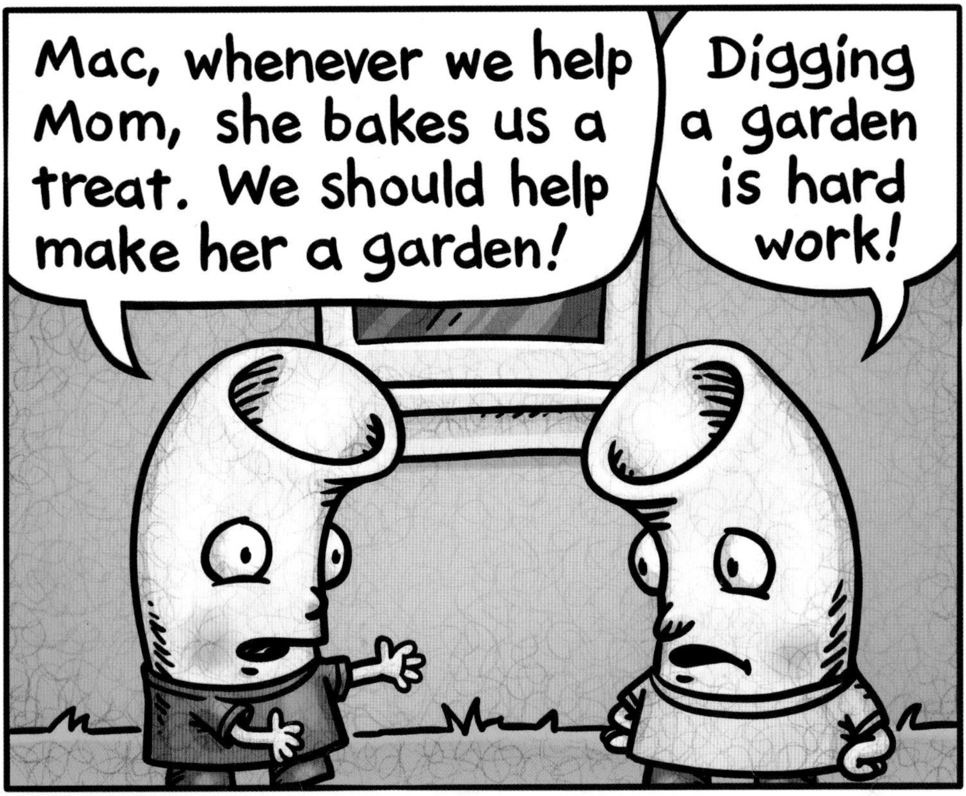
Mac, whenever we help Mom, she bakes us a treat. We should help make her a garden!
Digging a garden is hard work!

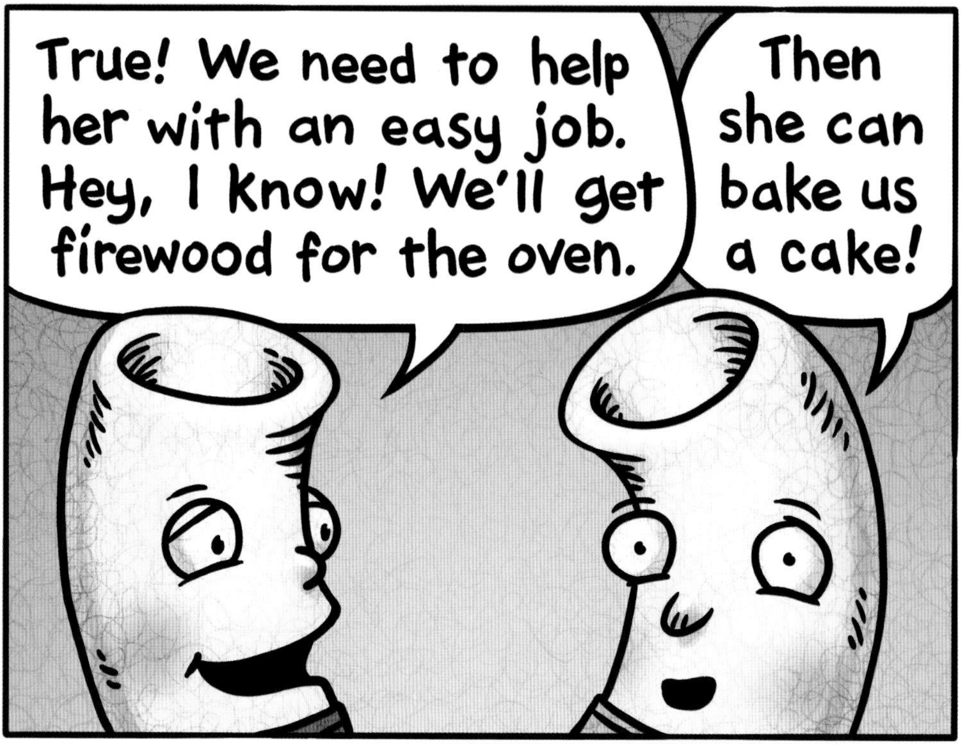
True! We need to help her with an easy job. Hey, I know! We'll get firewood for the oven.
Then she can bake us a cake!

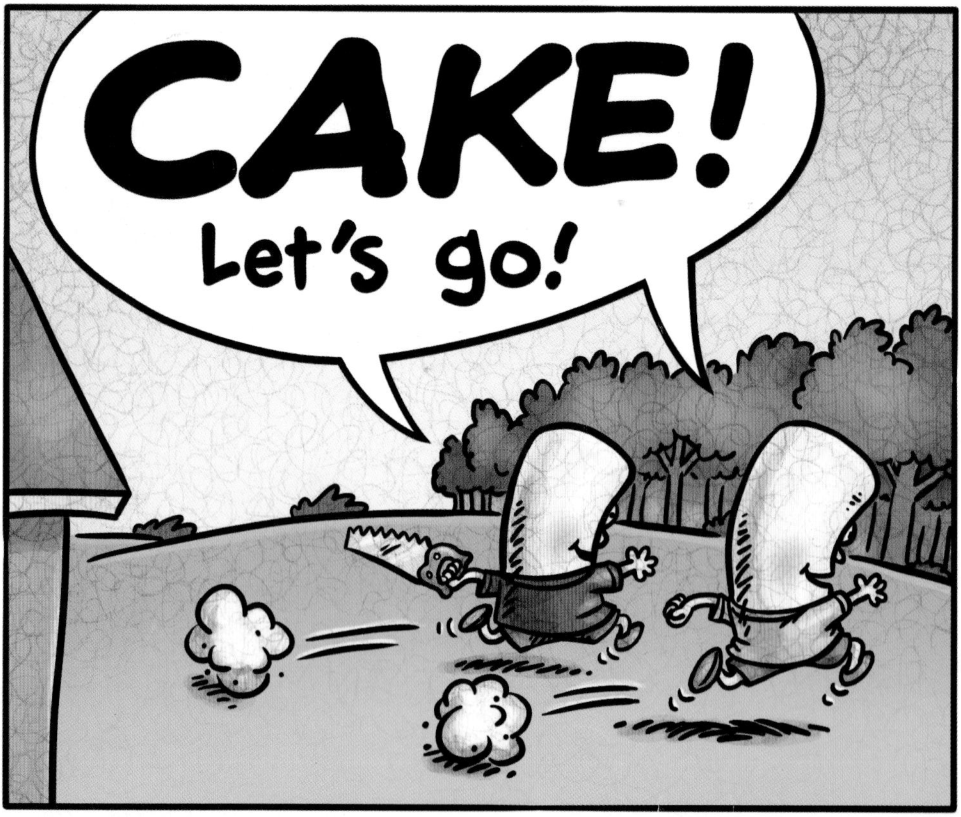
CAKE! Let's go!

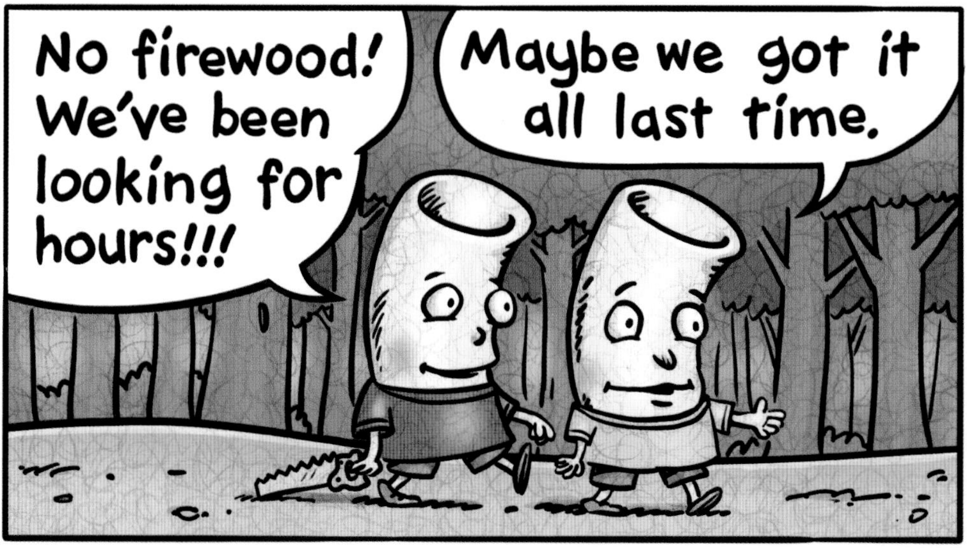
No firewood! We've been looking for hours!!!
Maybe we got it all last time.

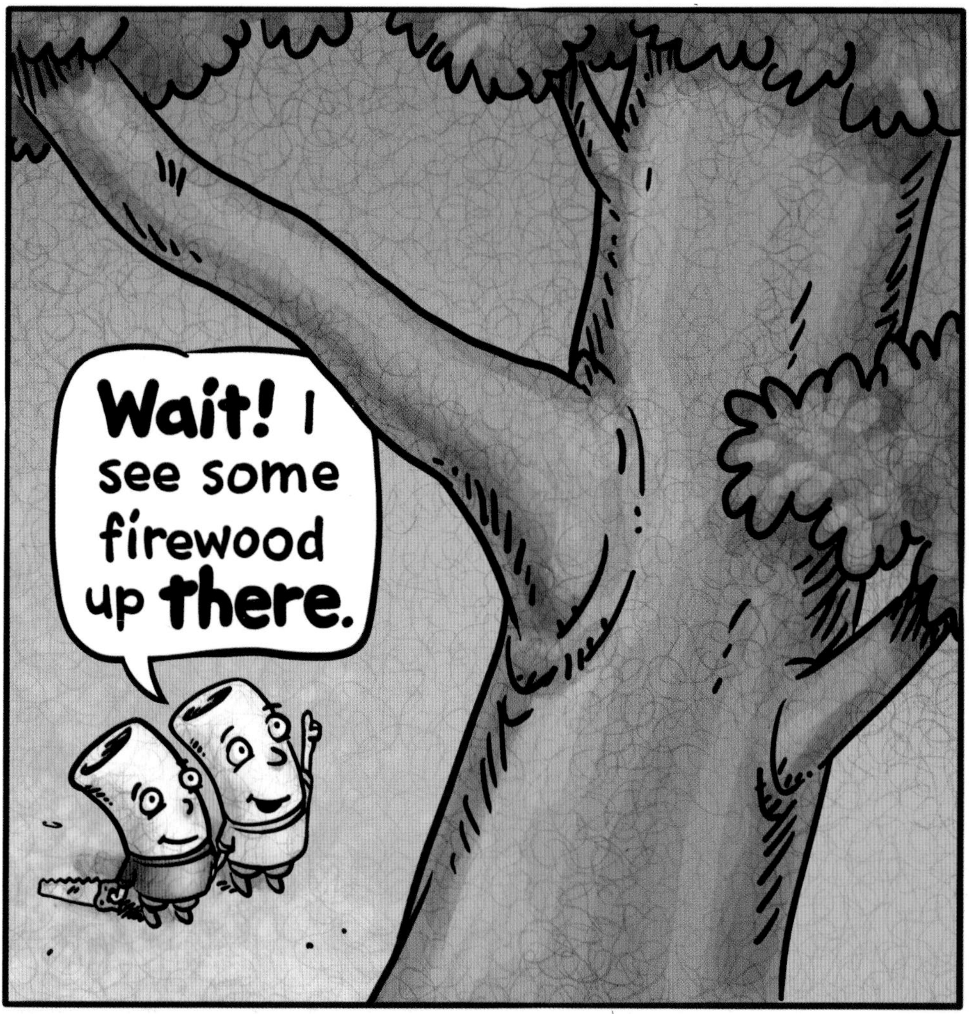
Wait! I see some firewood up there.

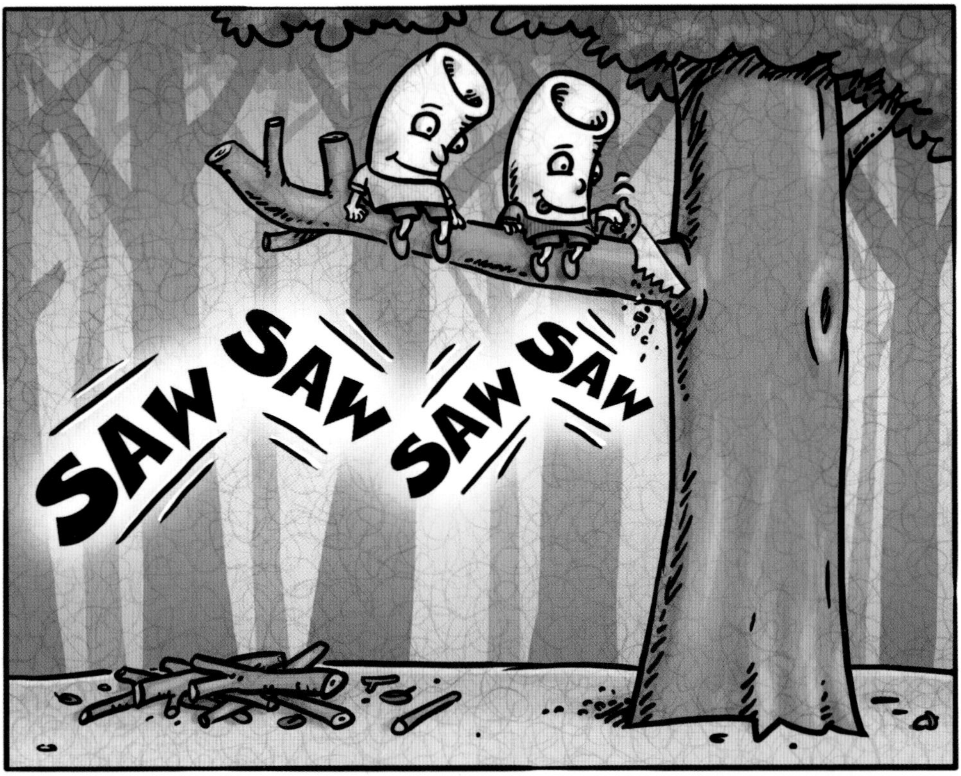
SAW SAW SAW SAW

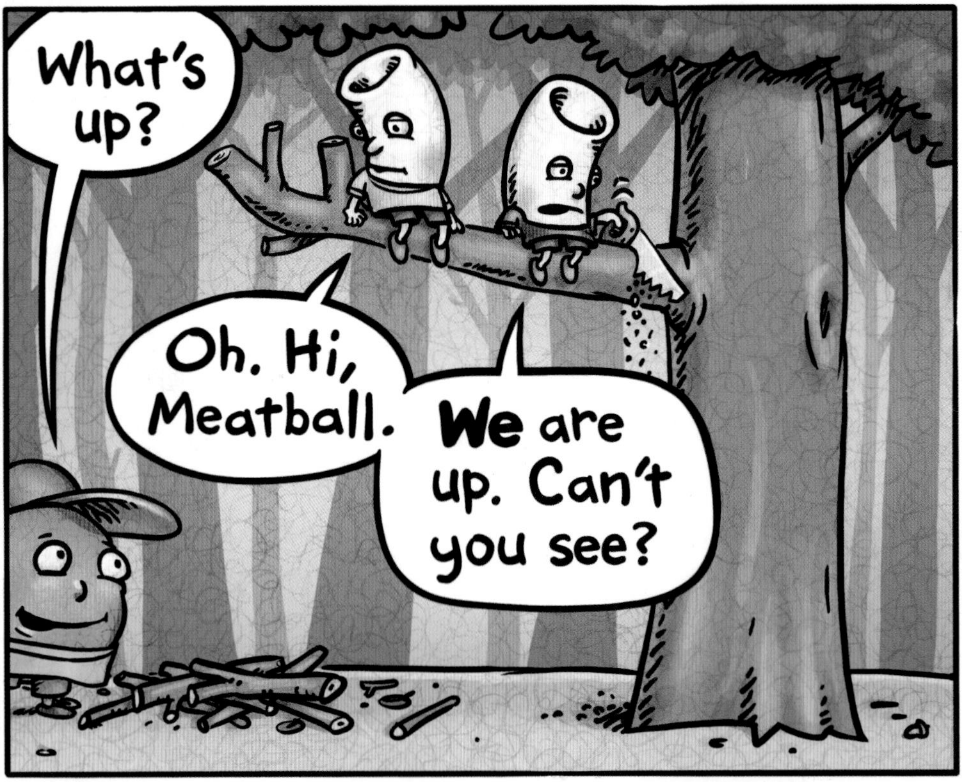
What's up?
Oh. Hi, Meatball.
We are up. Can't you see?

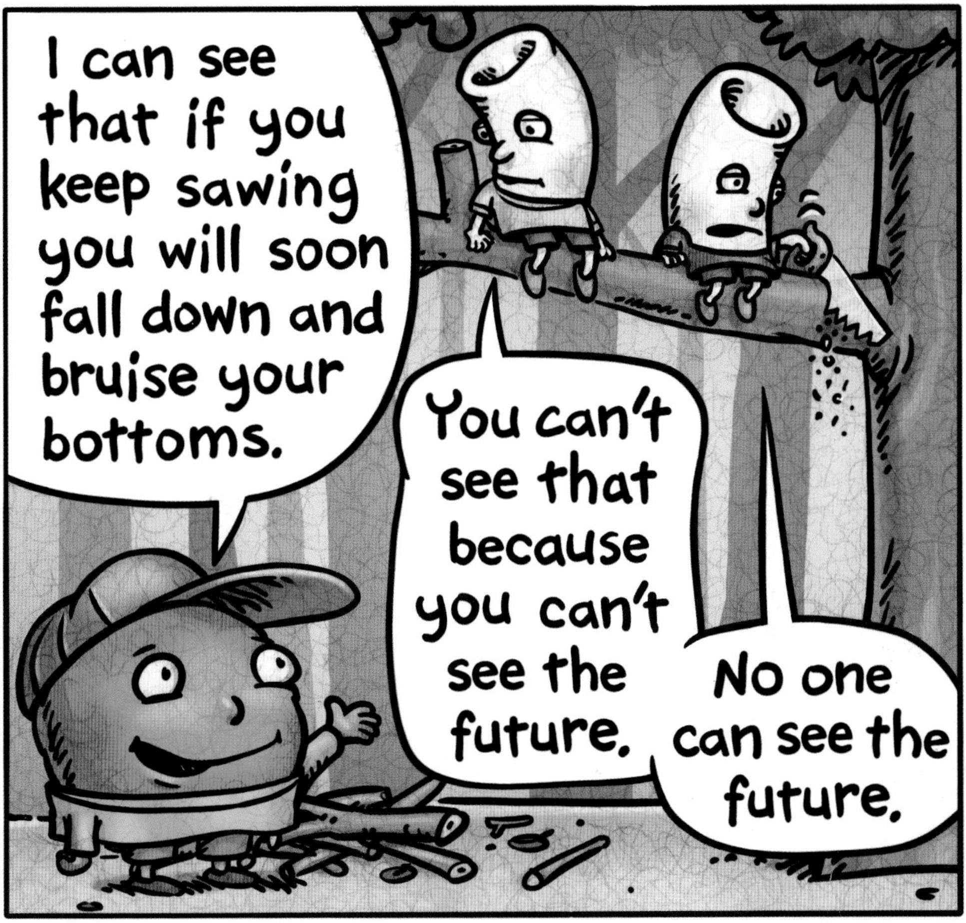
I can see that if you keep sawing you will soon fall down and bruise your bottoms.
You can't see that because you can't see the future.
No one can see the future.

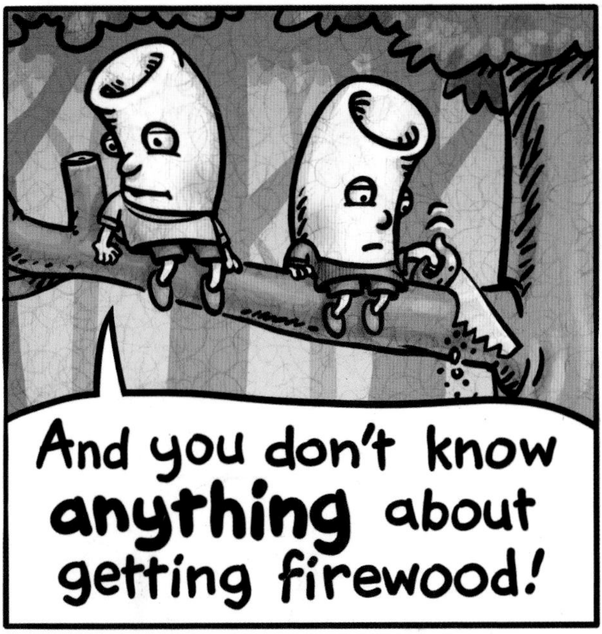
And you don't know **anything** about getting firewood!

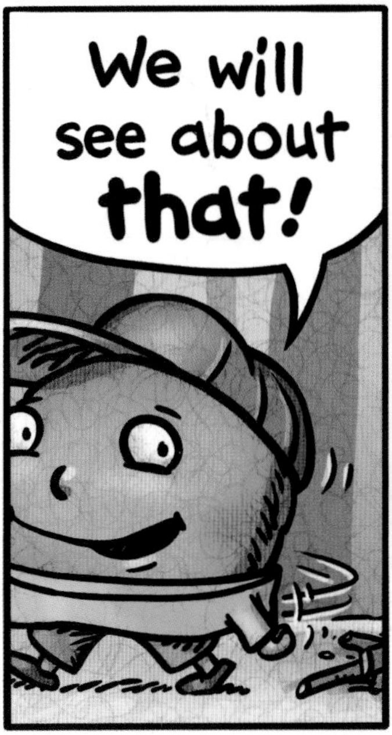
We will see about **that!**

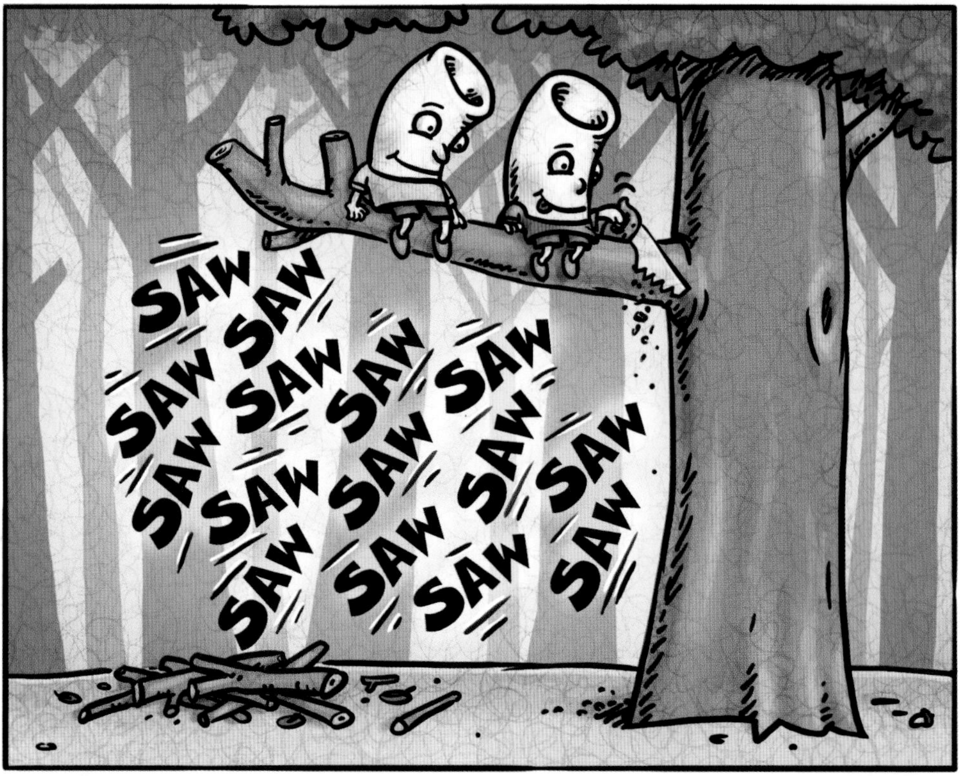
SAW SAW SAW SAW SAW SAW SAW SAW SAW SAW SAW SAW SAW SAW SAW SAW SAW SAW

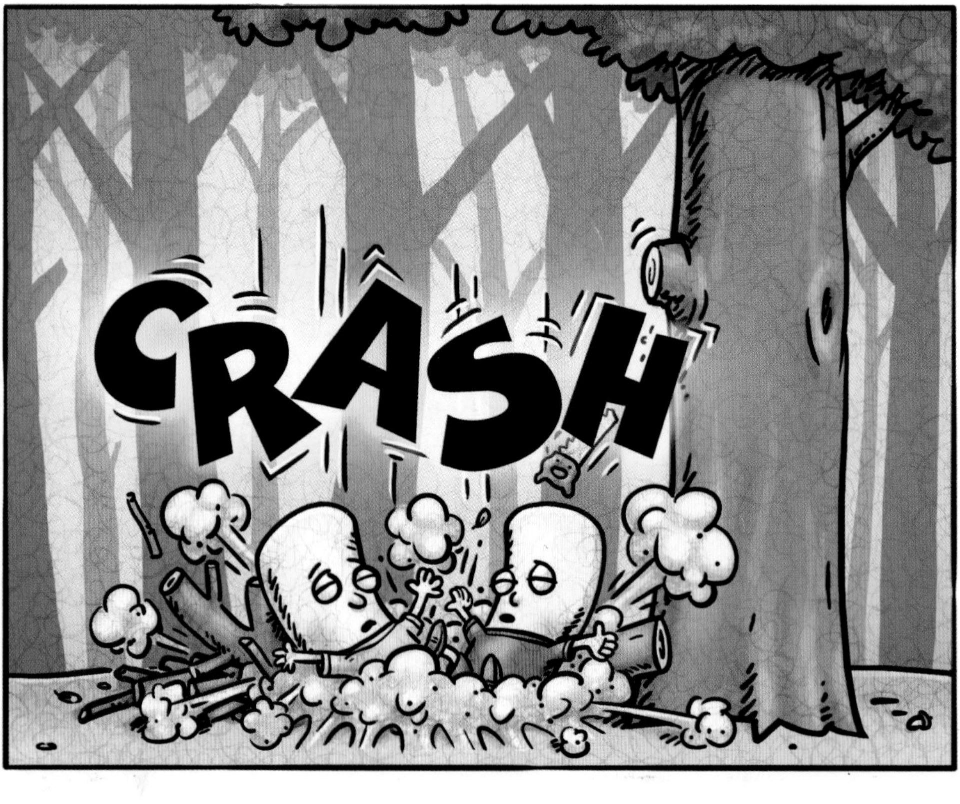
CRASH

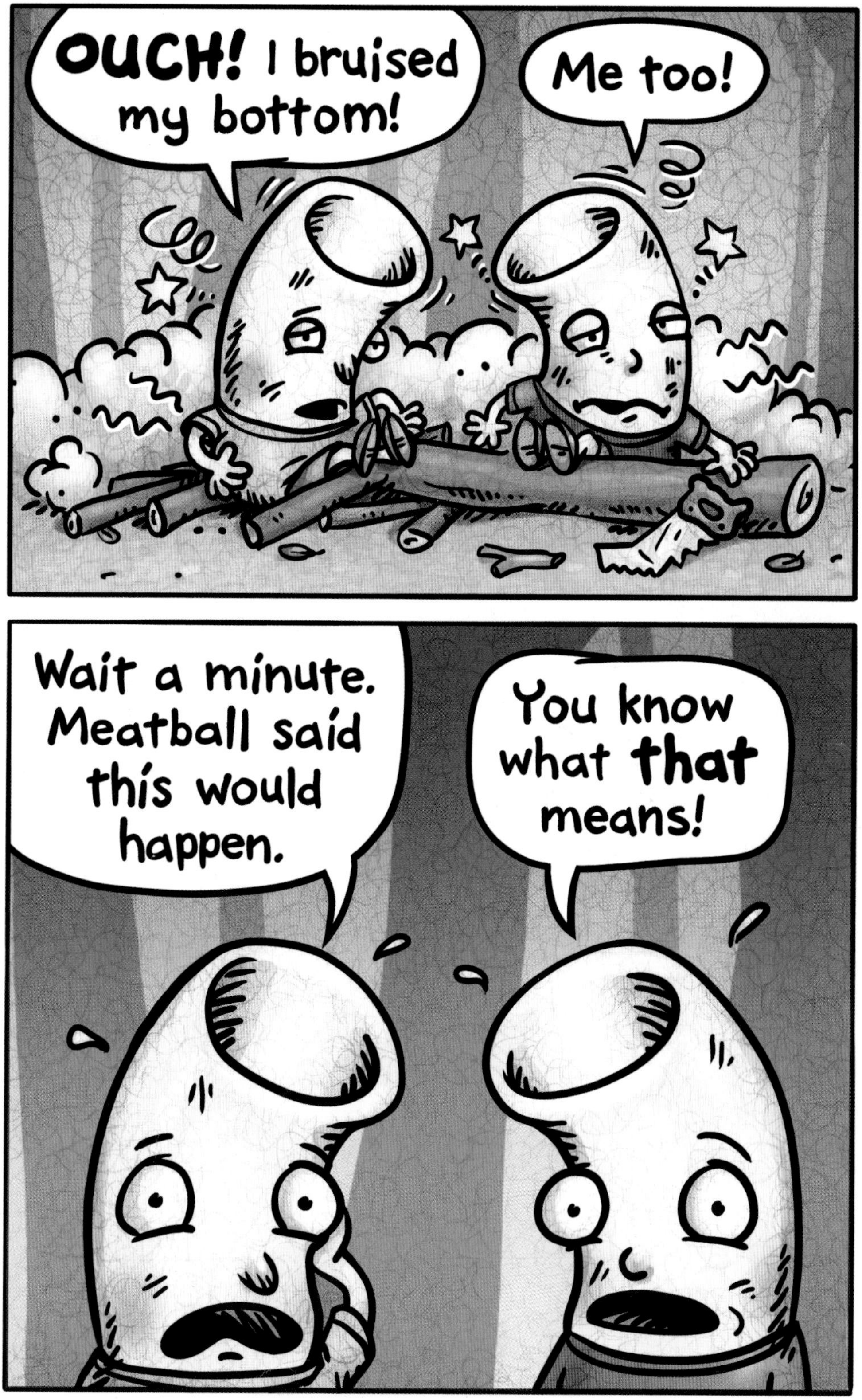
OUCH! I bruised my bottom!
Me too!
Wait a minute. Meatball said this would happen.
You know what **that** means!

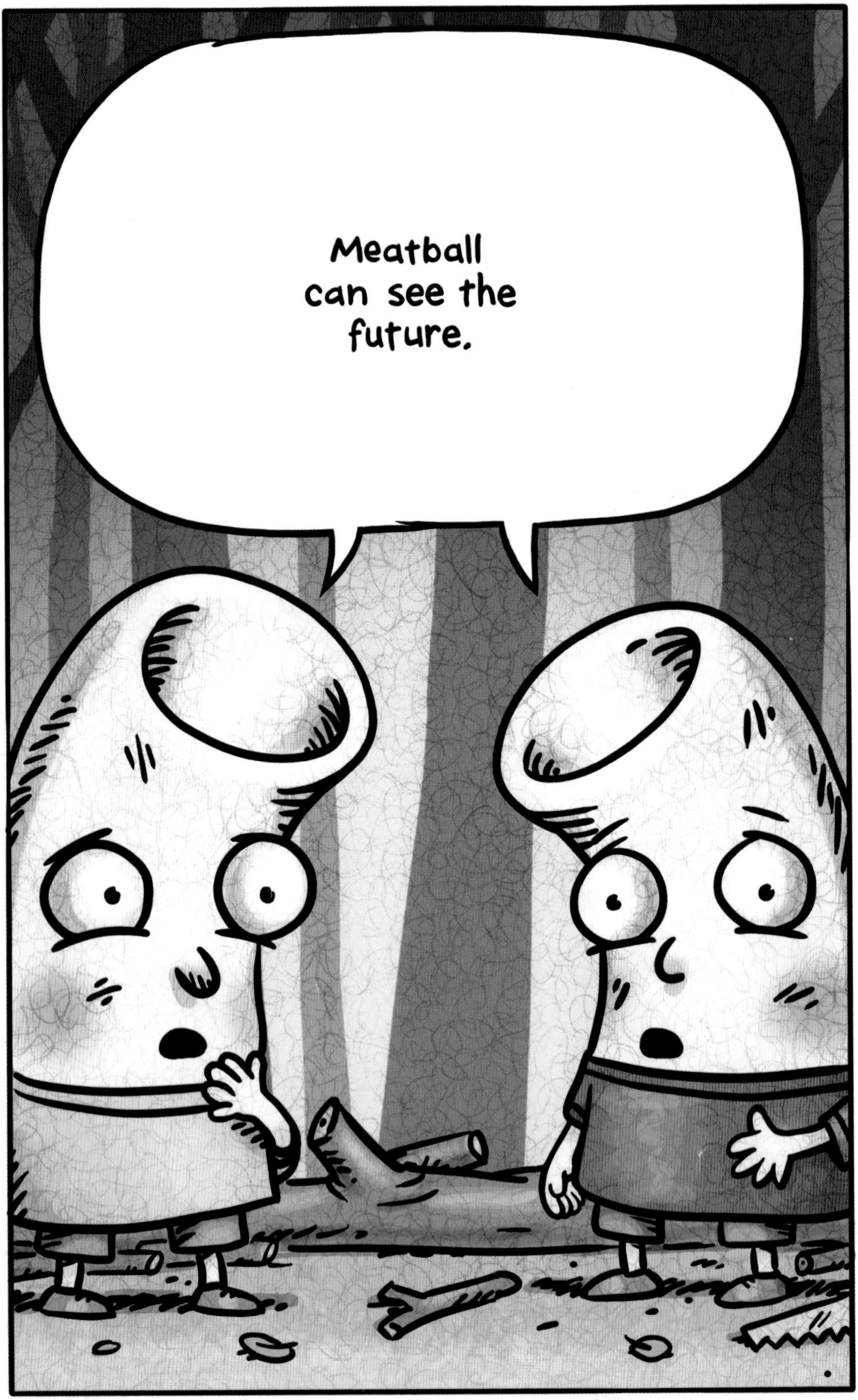
Meatball can see the future.

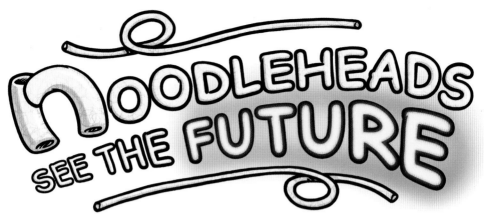

NOODLEHEADS SEE THE FUTURE

CHAPTER 2

THE TALKING DEAD

Meatball must be a fortune-teller!
I wonder what else he can see in our future.

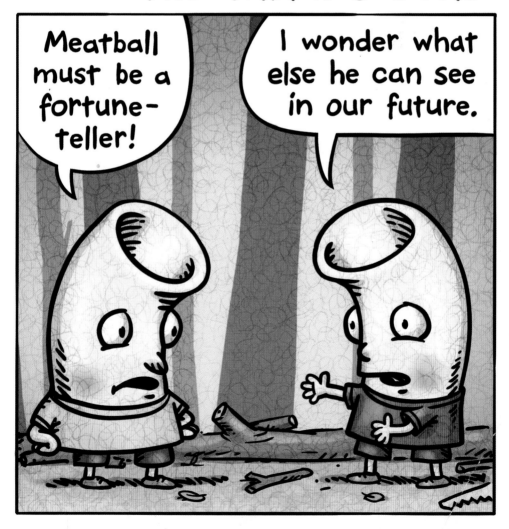

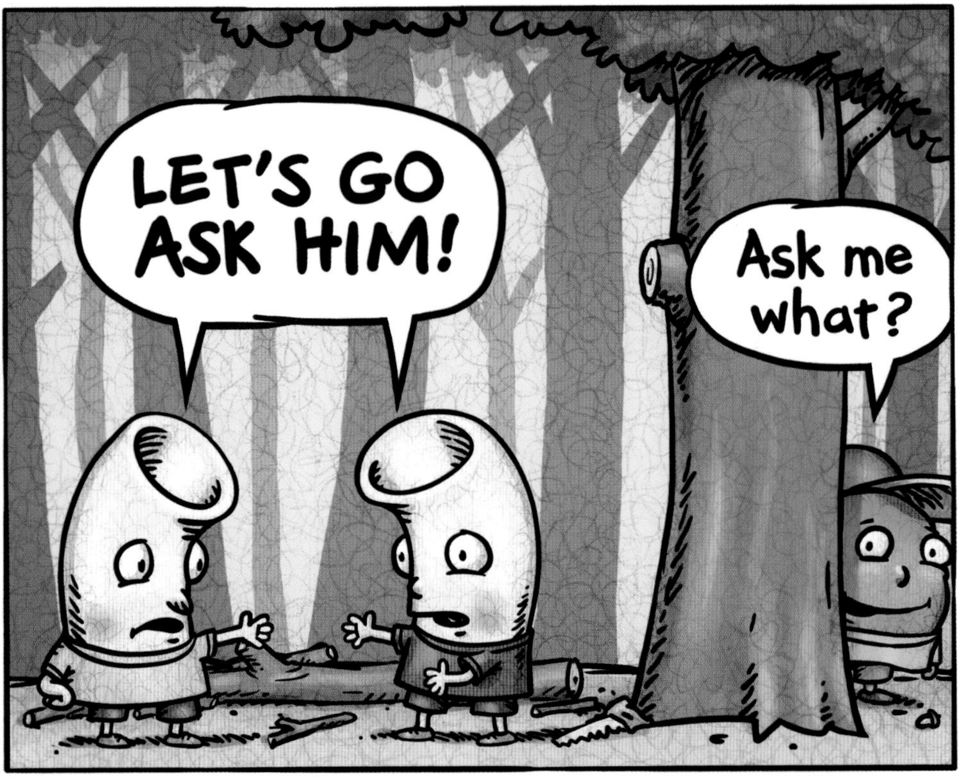
LET'S GO ASK HIM!
Ask me what?

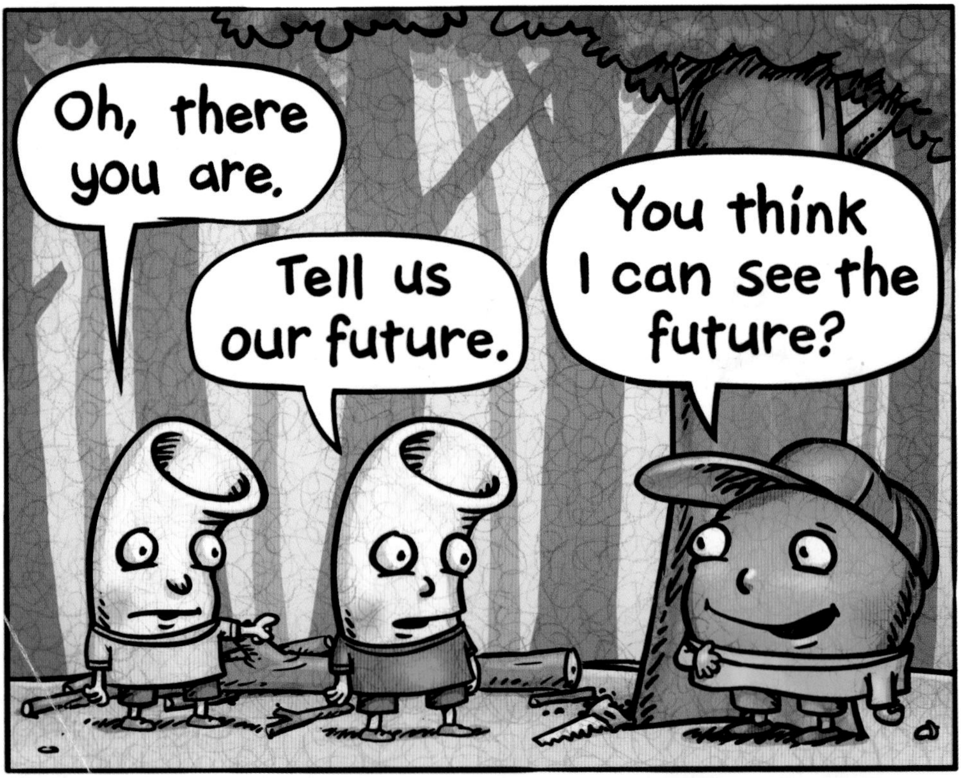
Oh, there you are.
Tell us our future.
You think I can see the future?

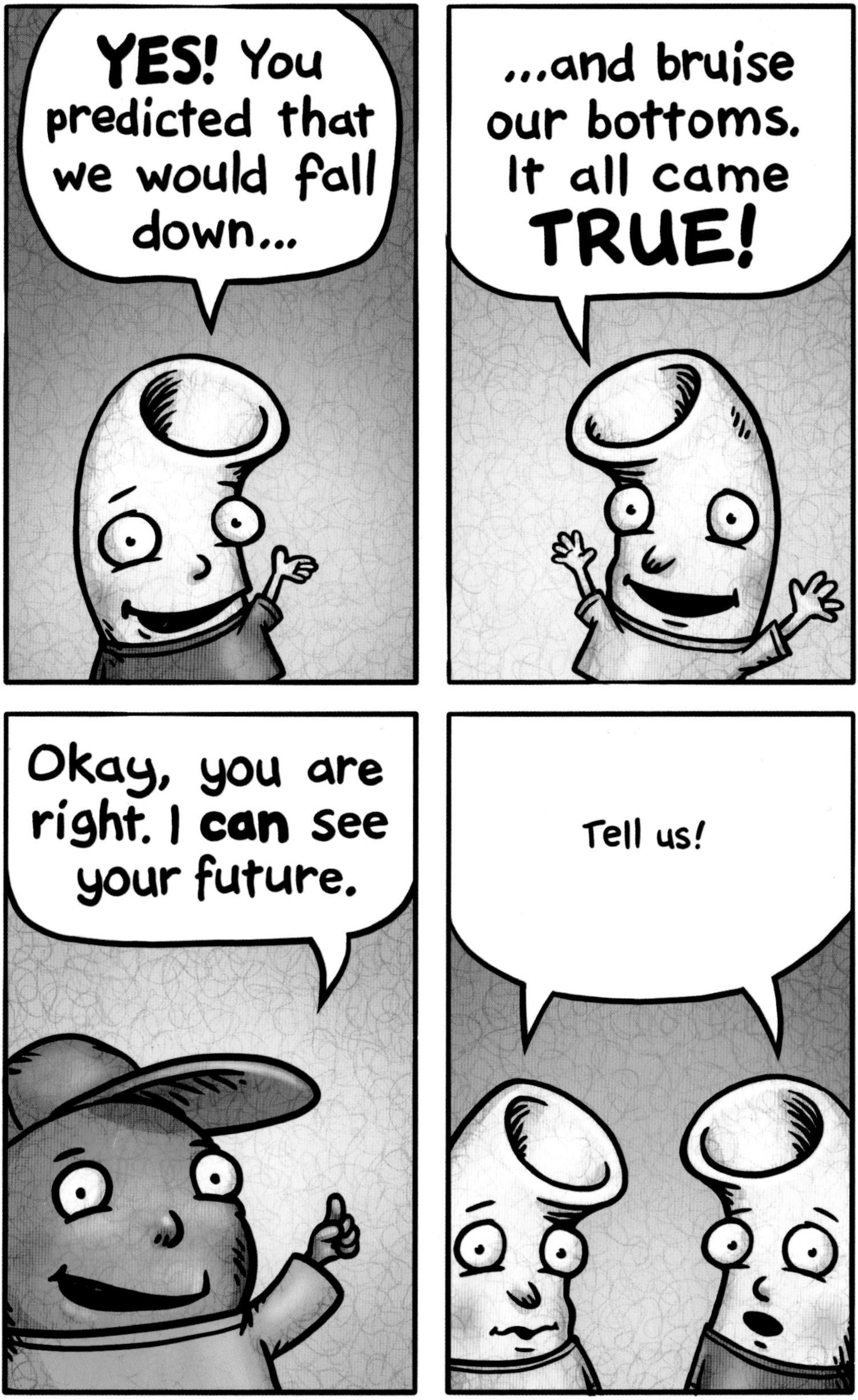
YES! You predicted that we would fall down...
...and bruise our bottoms. It all came TRUE!
Okay, you are right. I can see your future.
Tell us!

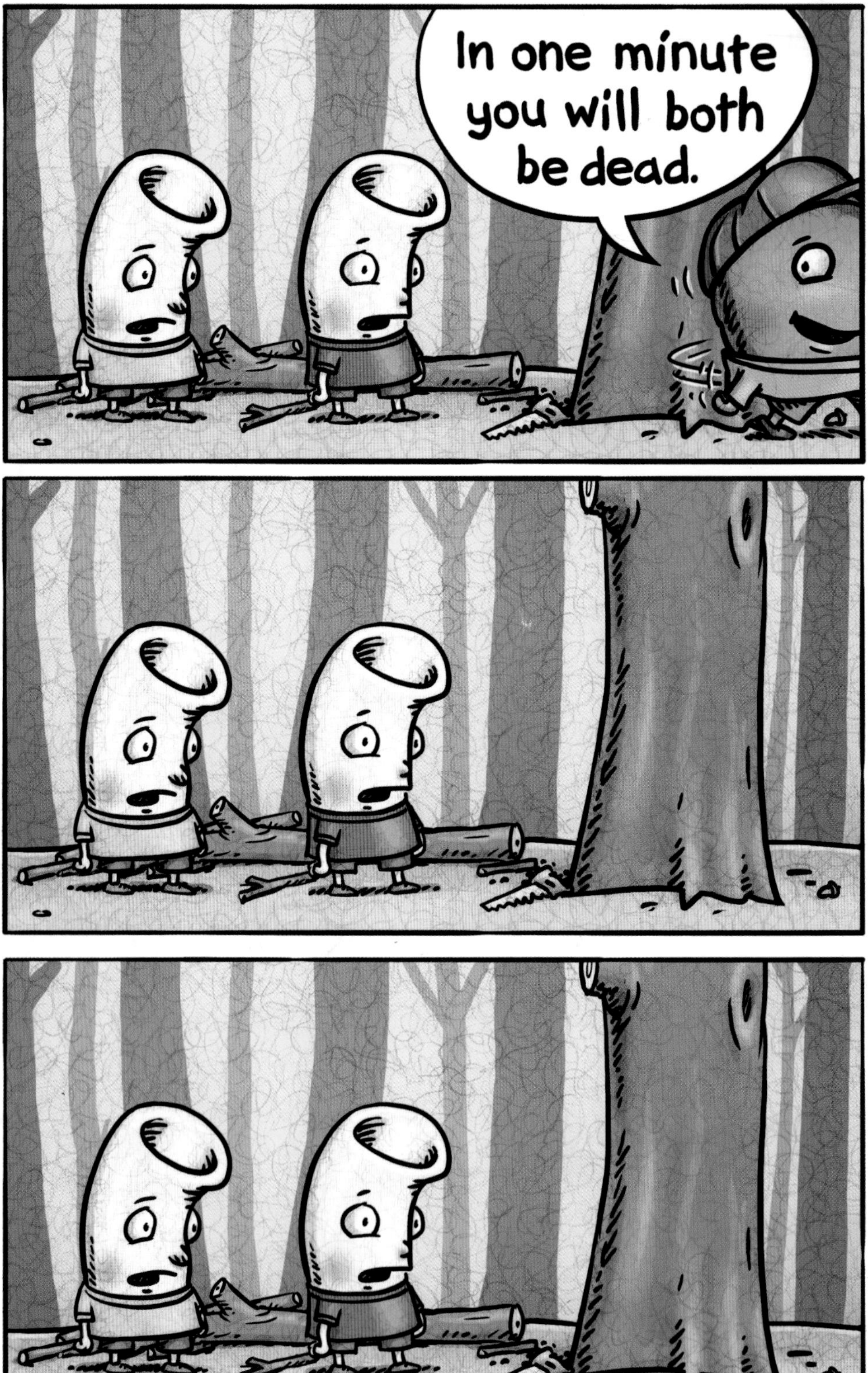
In one minute you will both be dead.

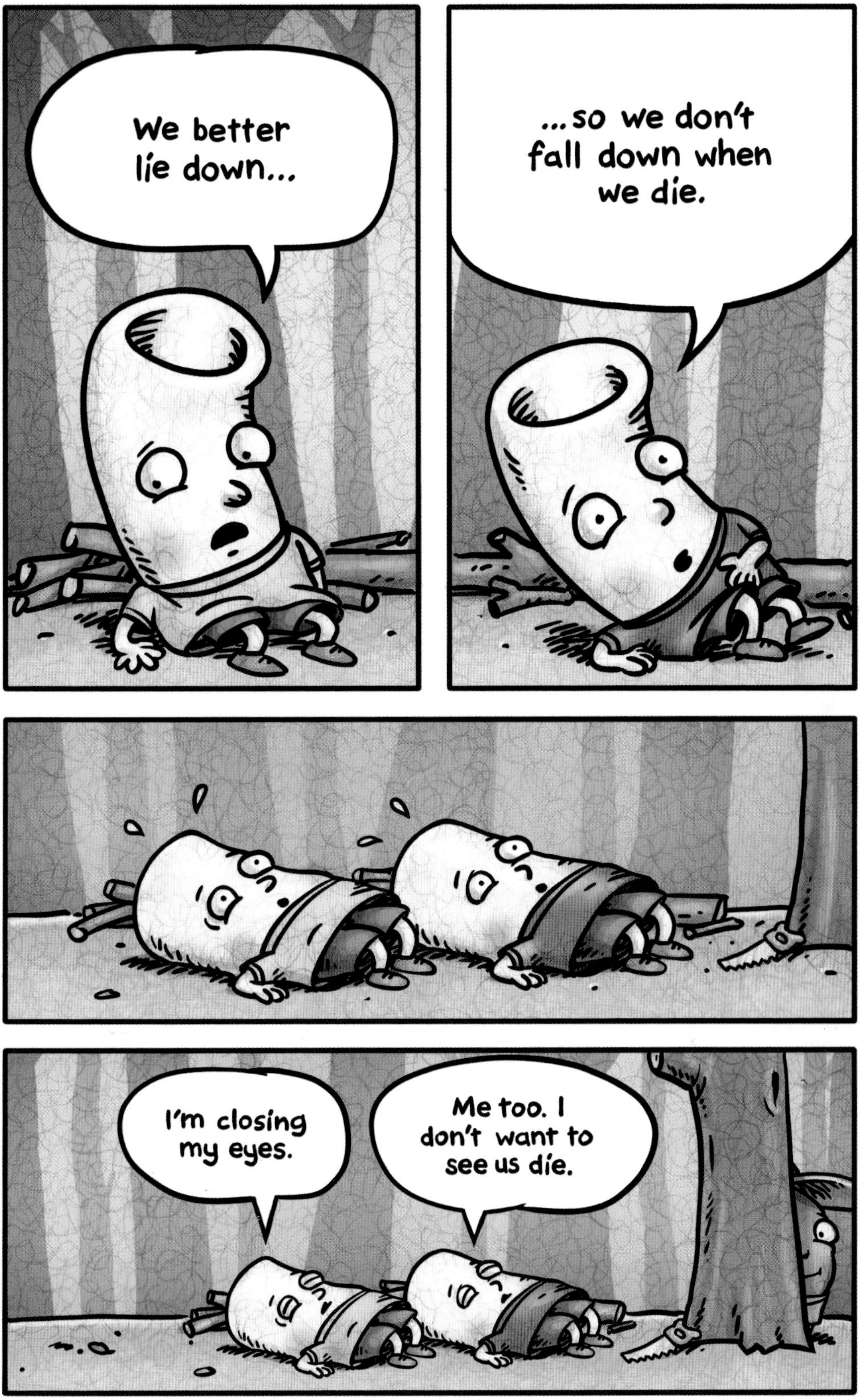
We better lie down...
...so we don't fall down when we die.
I'm closing my eyes.
Me too. I don't want to see us die.

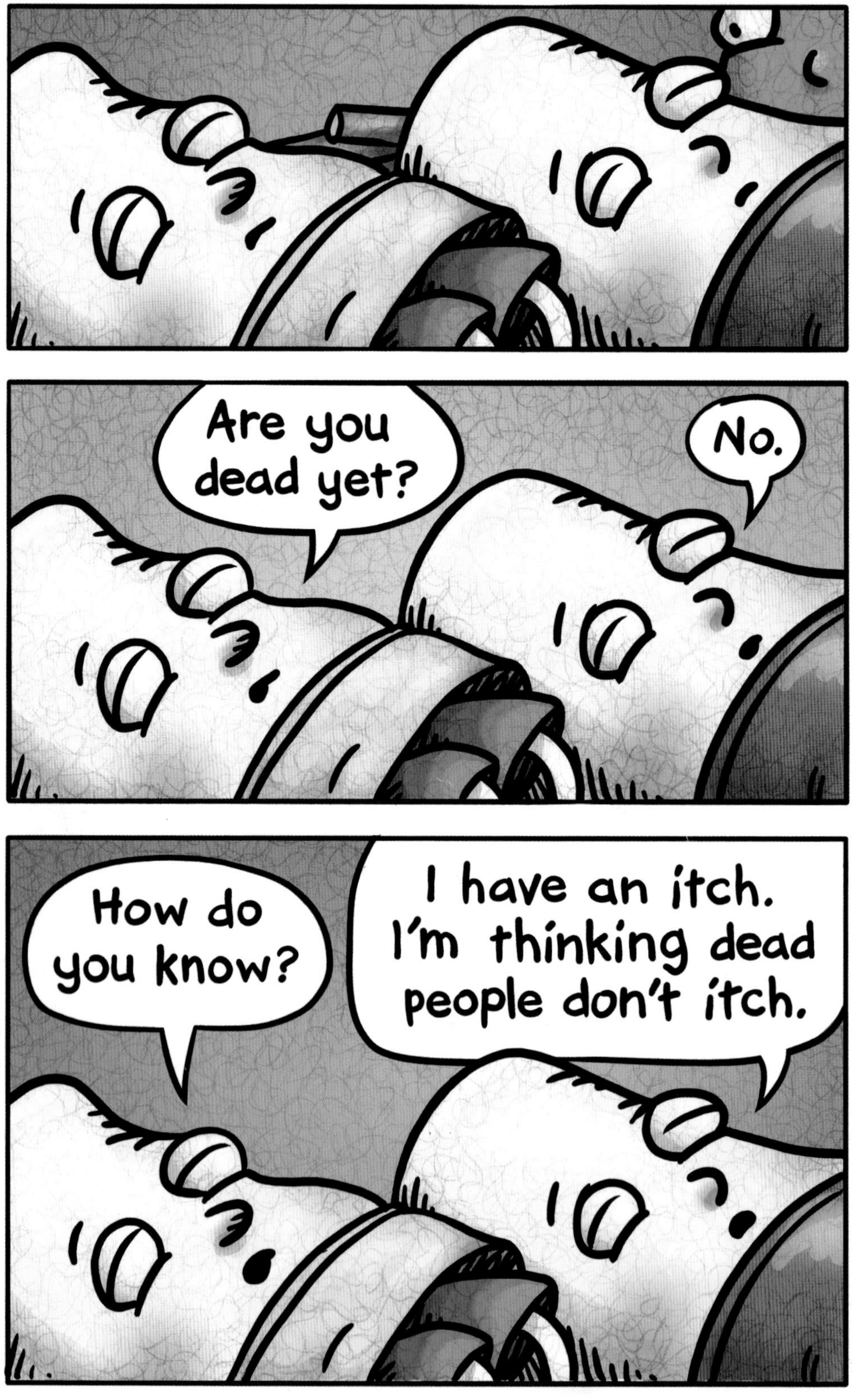
Are you dead yet?
No.
How do you know?
I have an itch. I'm thinking dead people don't itch.

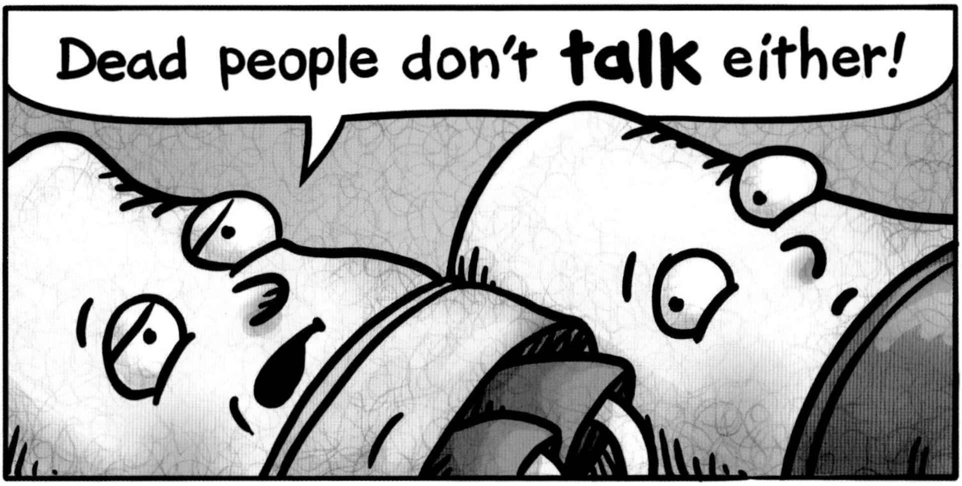
Dead people don't **talk** either!

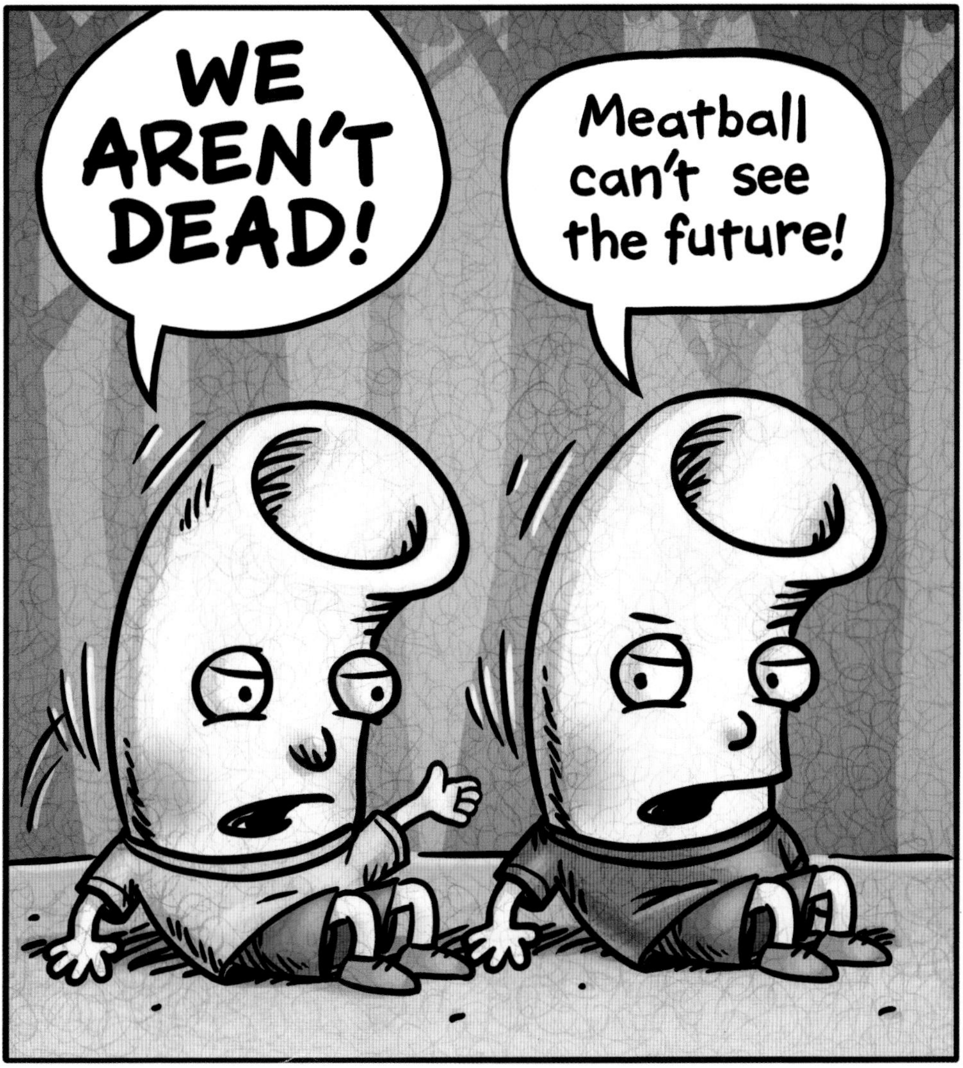
WE AREN'T DEAD!
Meatball can't see the future!

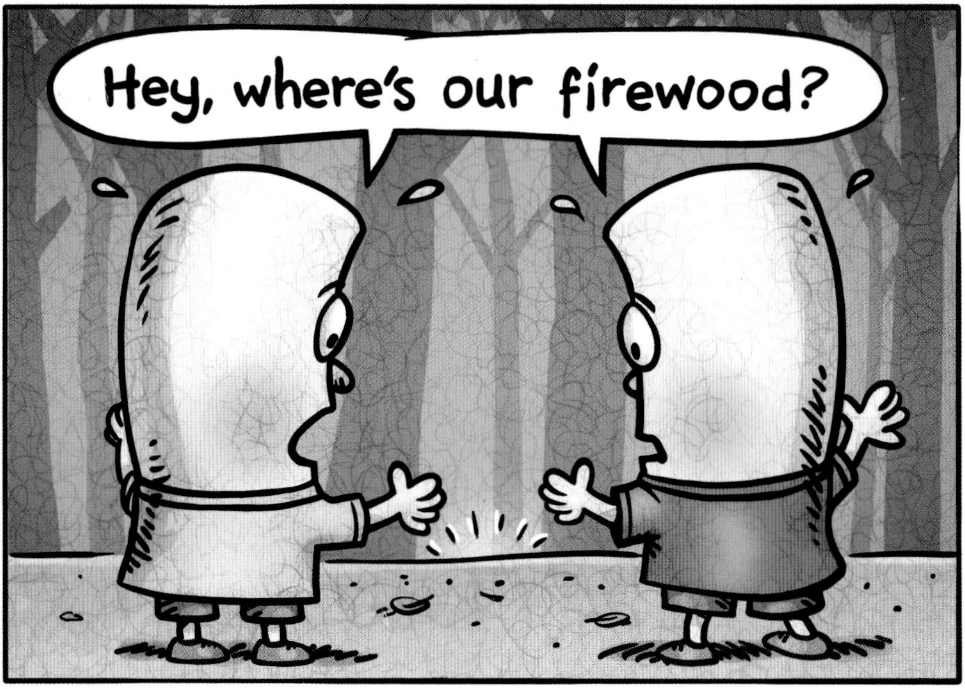
Hey, where's our firewood?

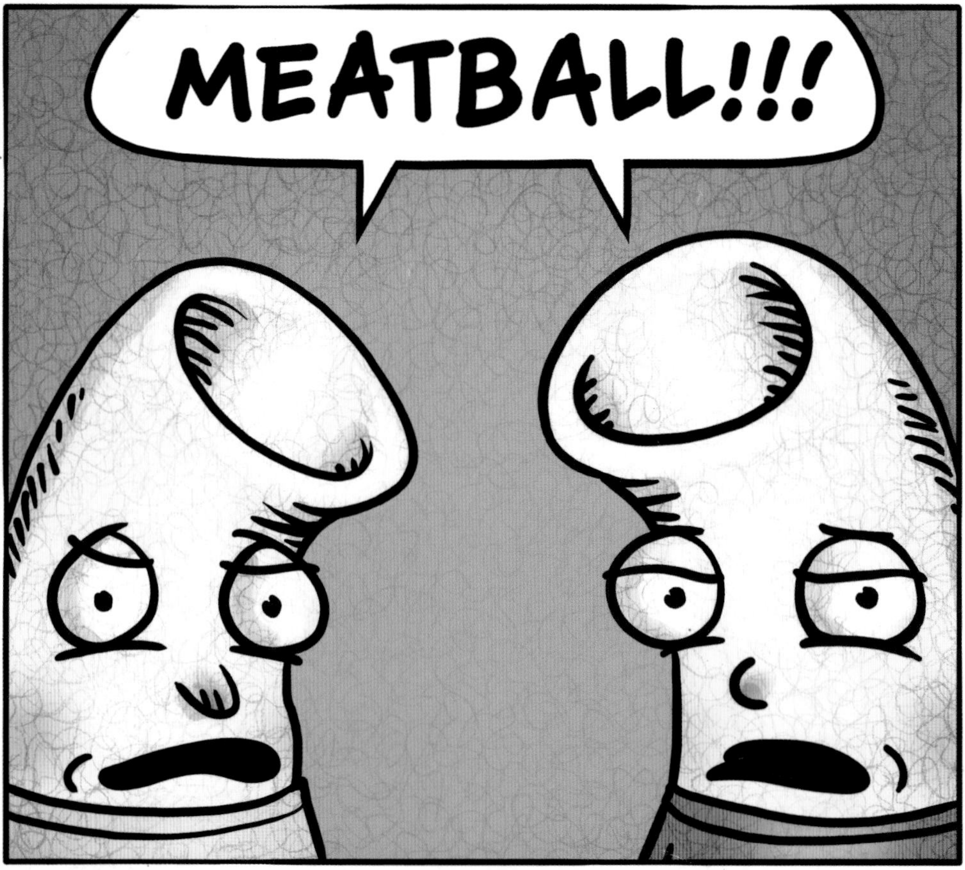
MEATBALL!!!

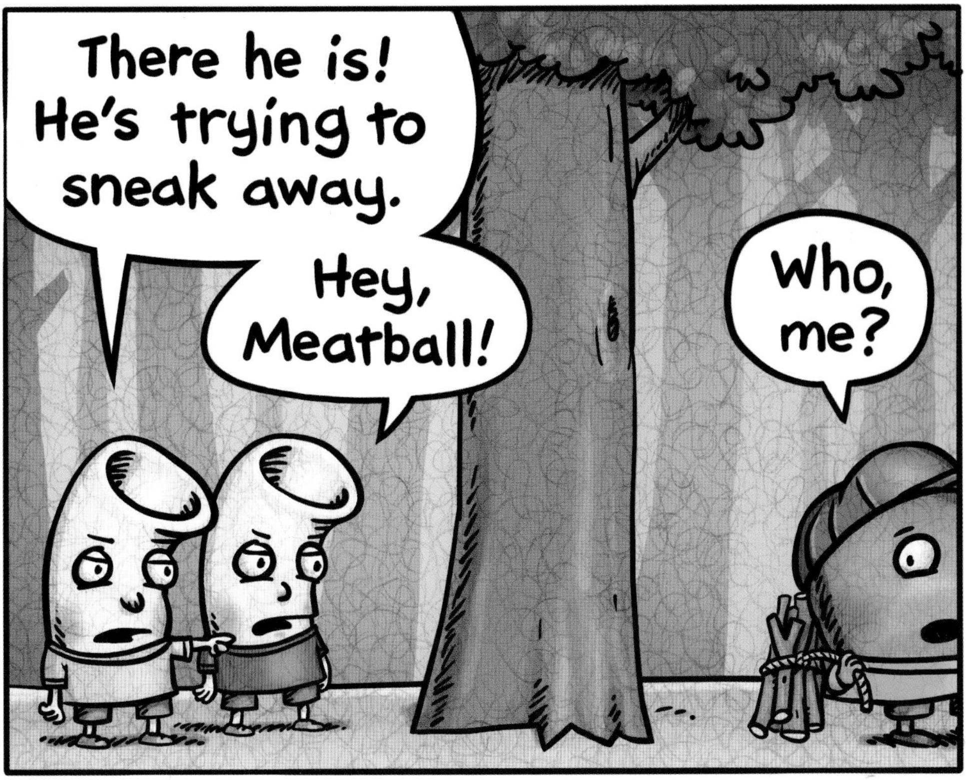
There he is! He's trying to sneak away.
Hey, Meatball!
Who, me?

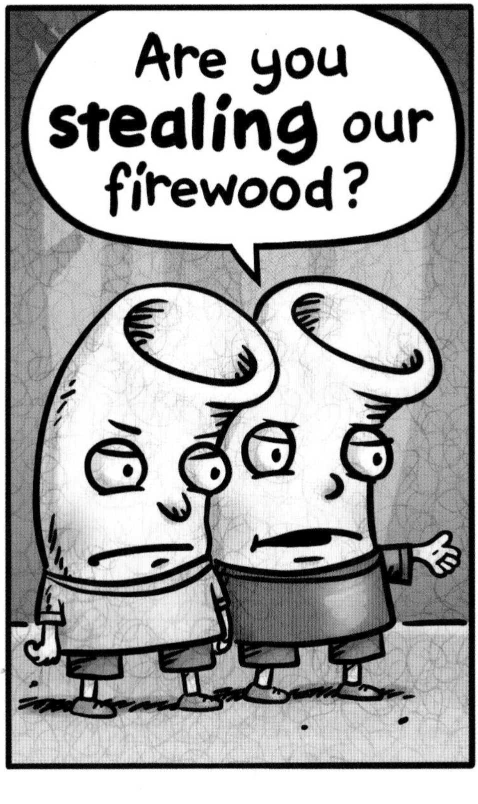
Are you **stealing** our firewood?

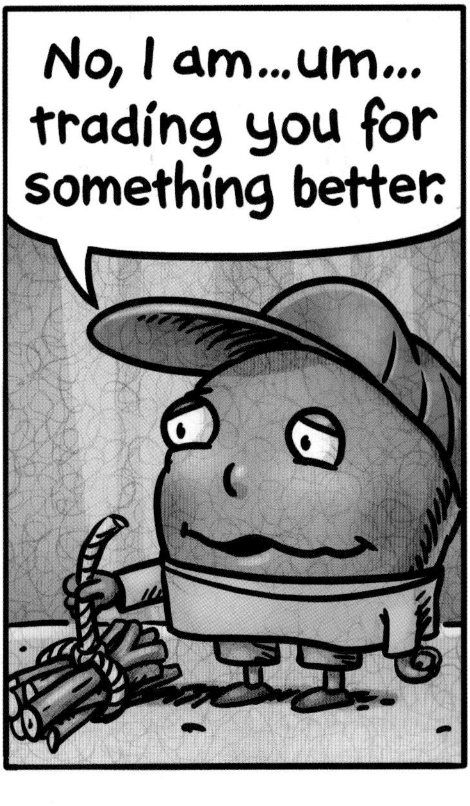
No, I am...um... trading you for something better.

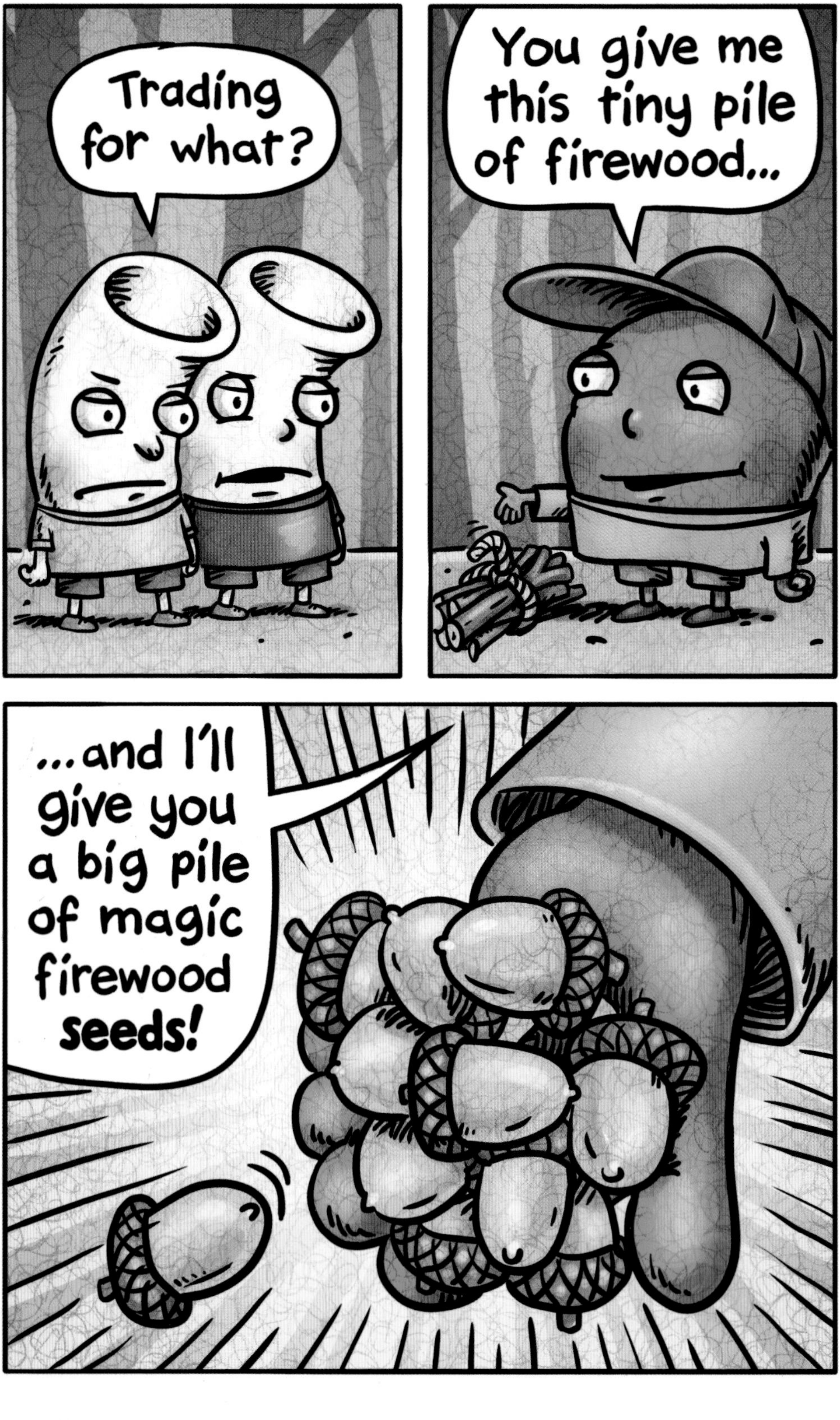
Trading for what?
You give me this tiny pile of firewood...
...and I'll give you a big pile of magic firewood seeds!

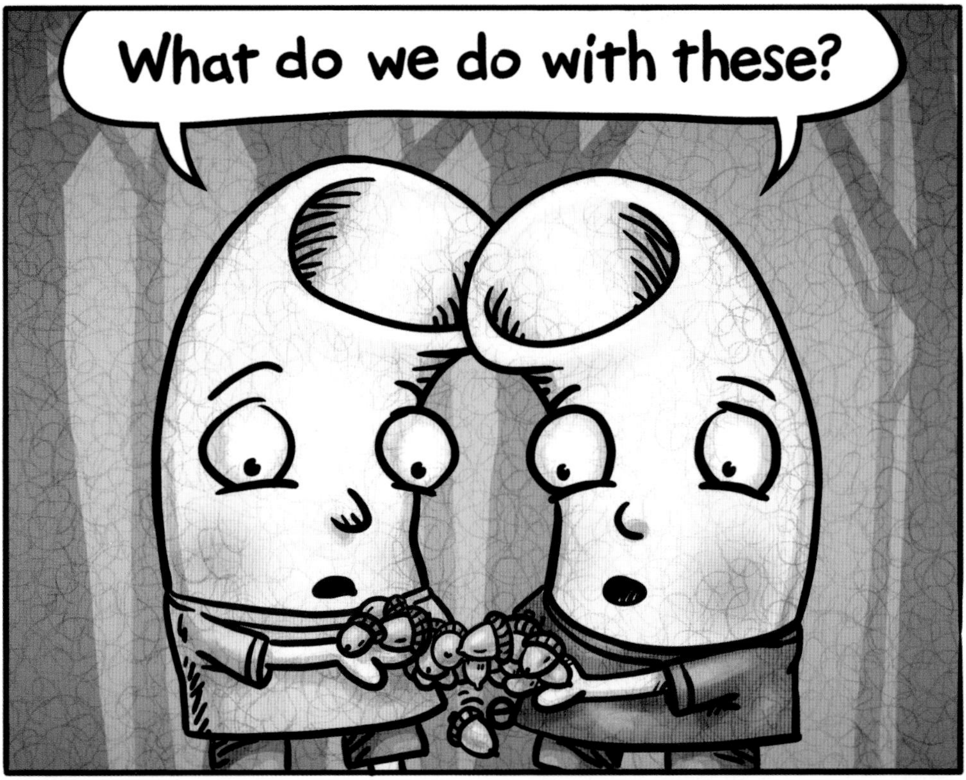
What do we do with these?

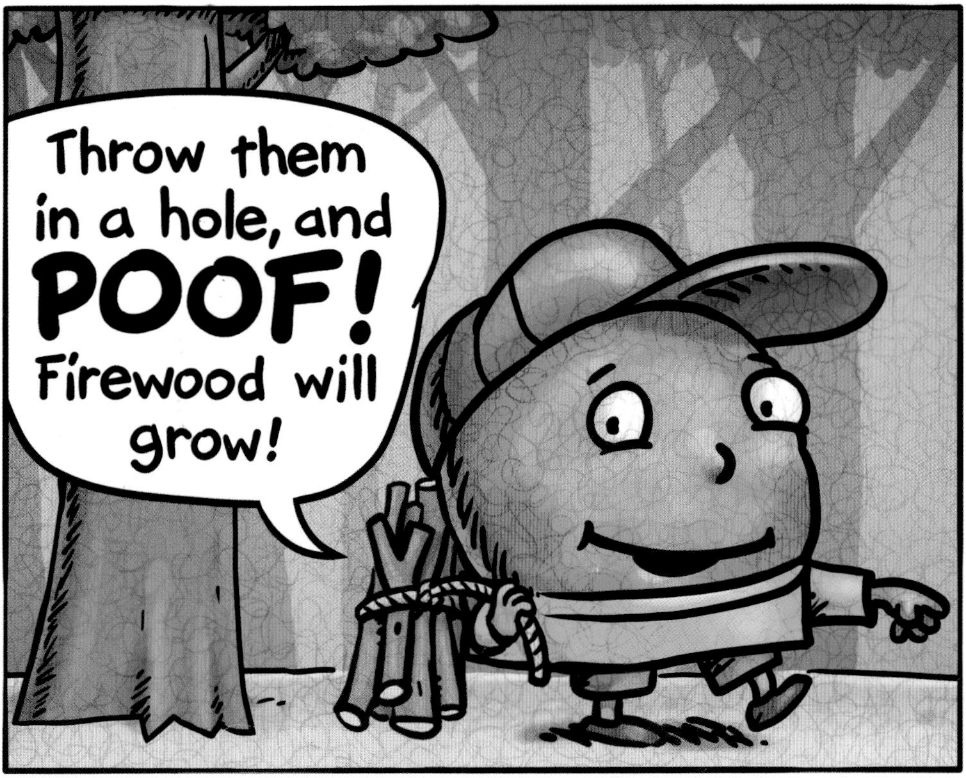
Throw them in a hole, and POOF! Firewood will grow!

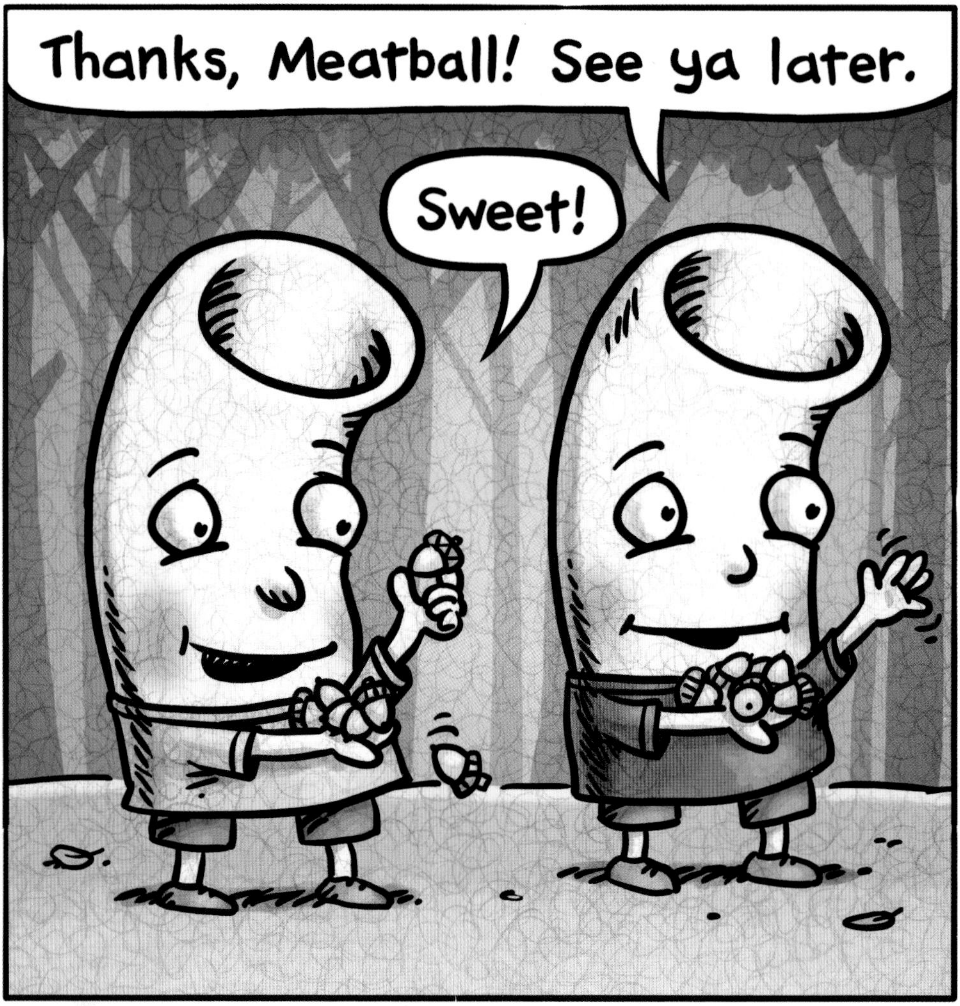
Thanks, Meatball! See ya later.
Sweet!

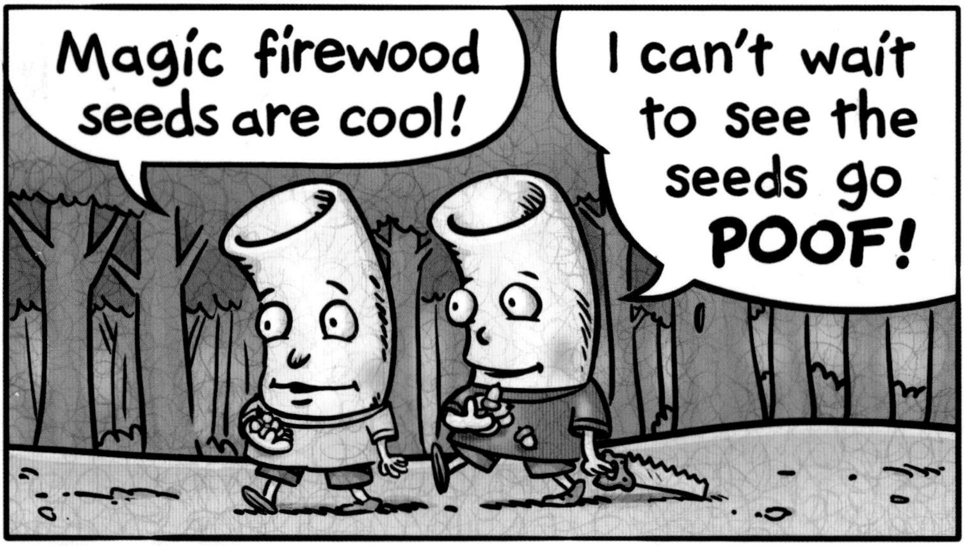
Magic firewood seeds are cool!
I can't wait to see the seeds go POOF!

NOODLEHEADS SEE THE FUTURE

CHAPTER 3

SEEING THE FUTURE

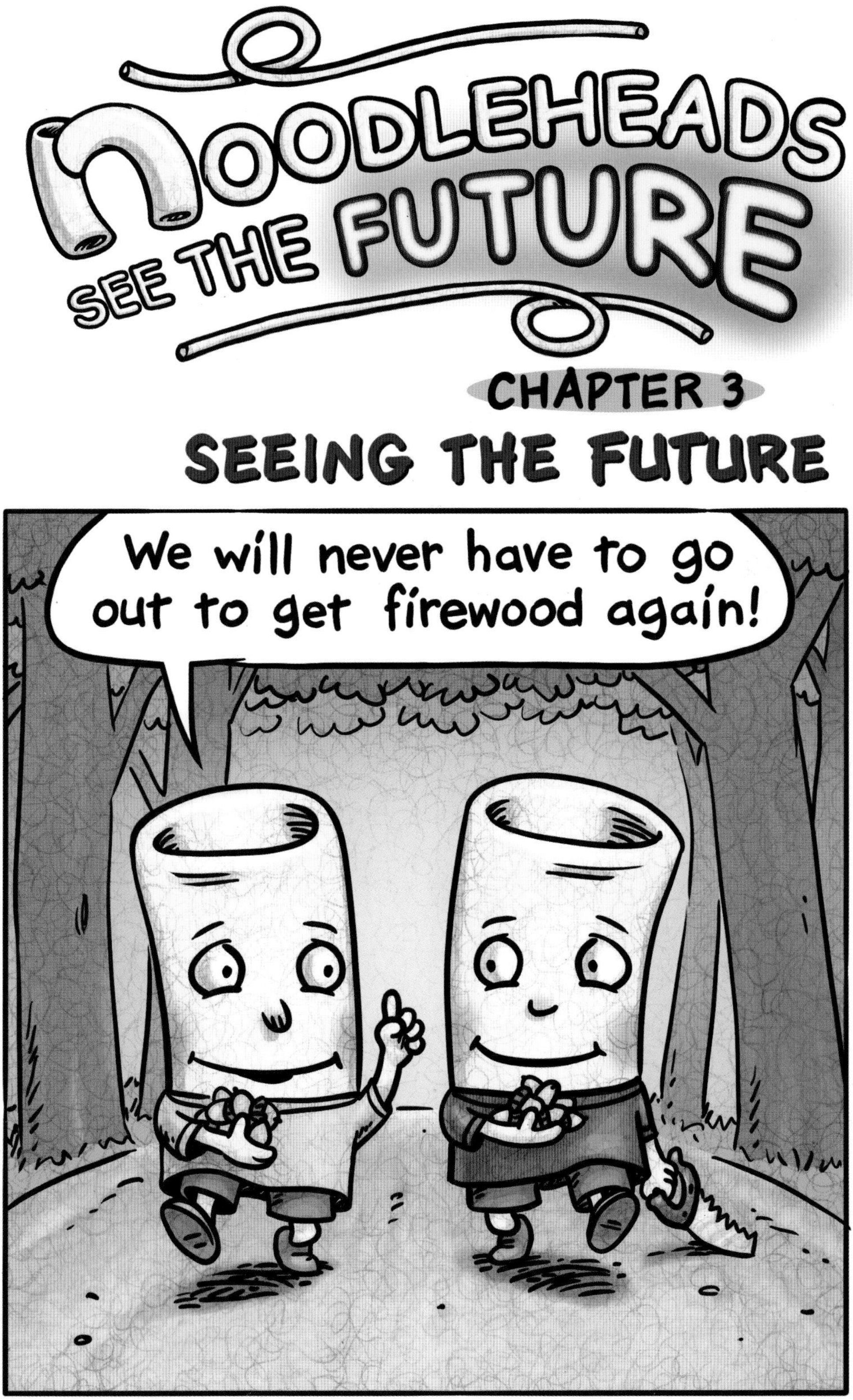
We will never have to go out to get firewood again!

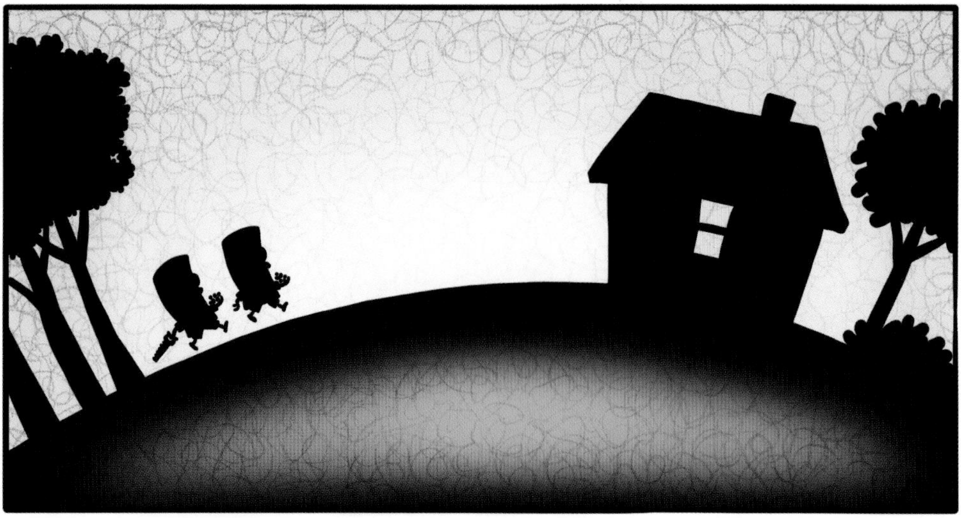

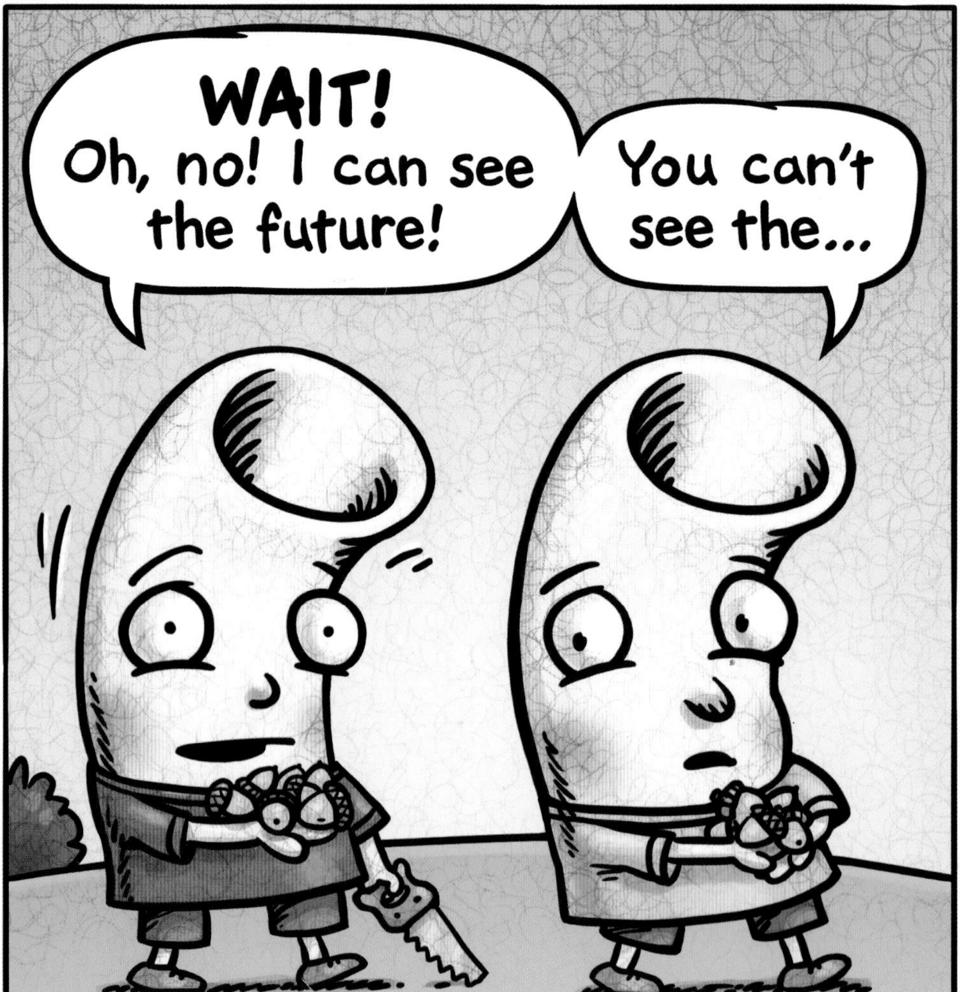
WAIT!
Oh, no! I can see the future!
You can't see the...

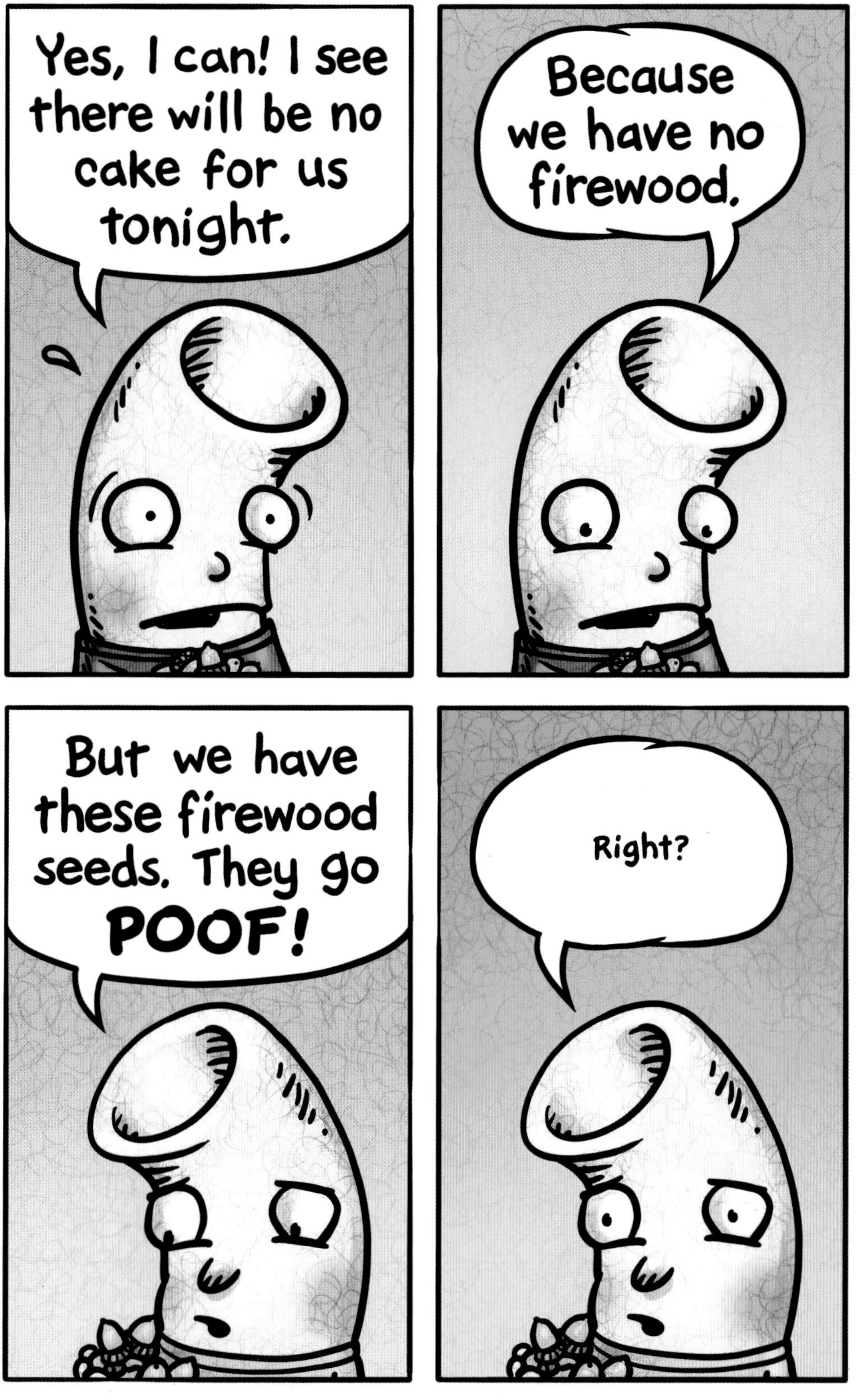
Yes, I can! I see there will be no cake for us tonight.
Because we have no firewood.
But we have these firewood seeds. They go POOF!
Right?

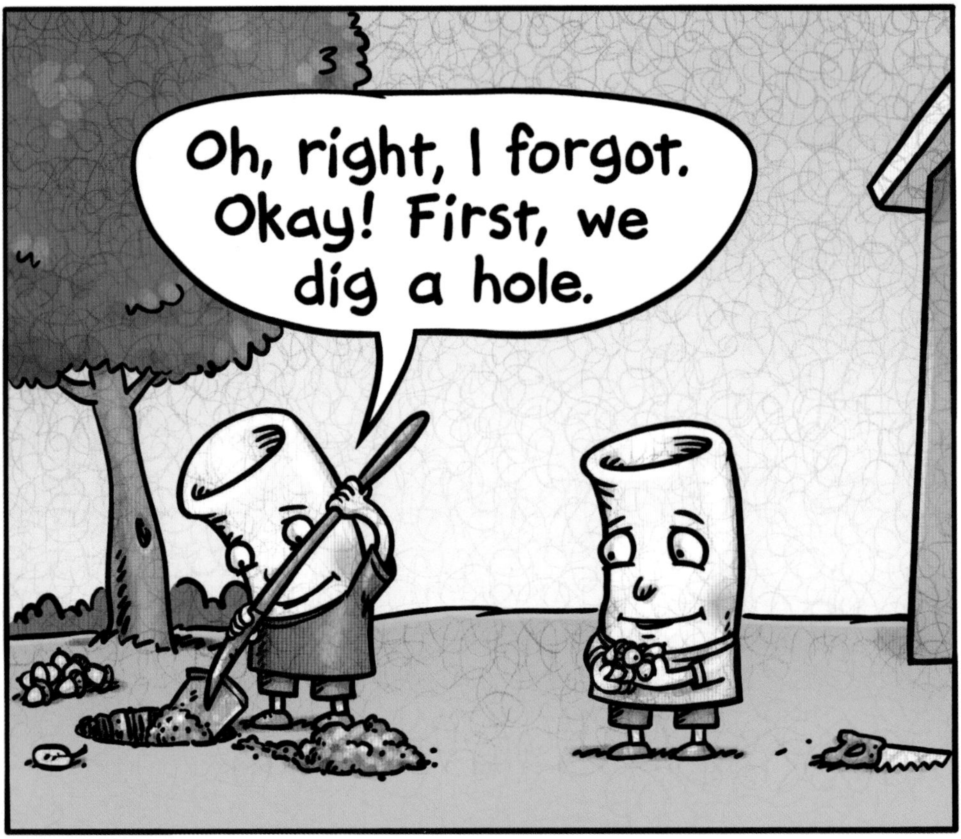
Oh, right, I forgot. Okay! First, we dig a hole.

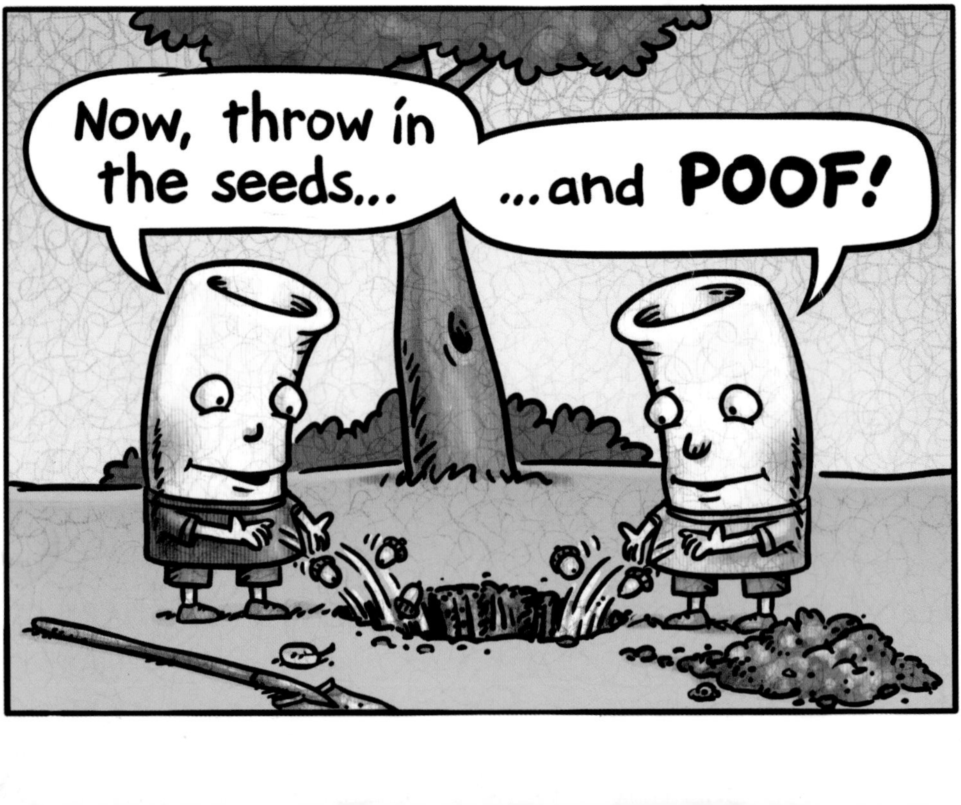
Now, throw in the seeds...
...and POOF!

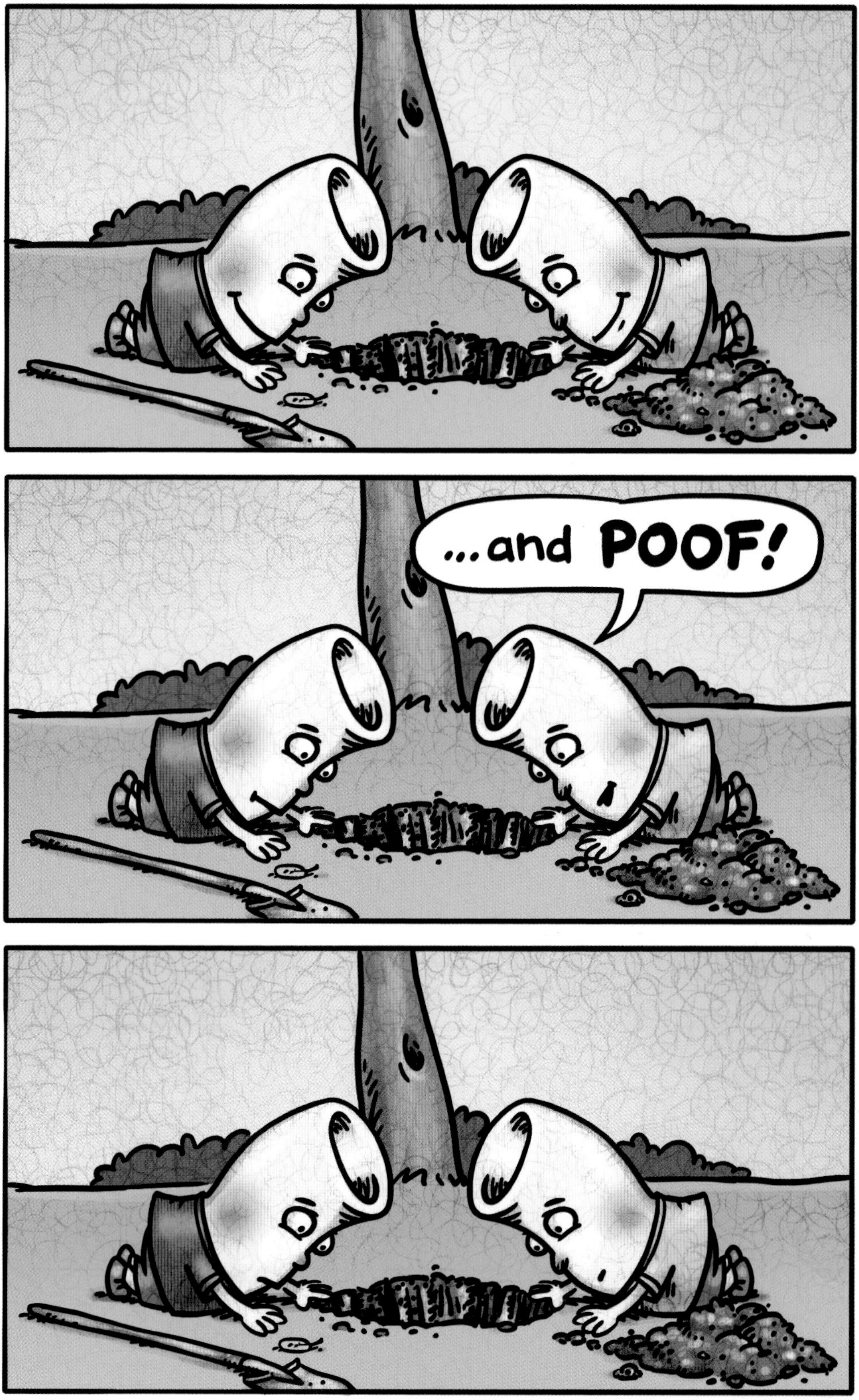
...and POOF!

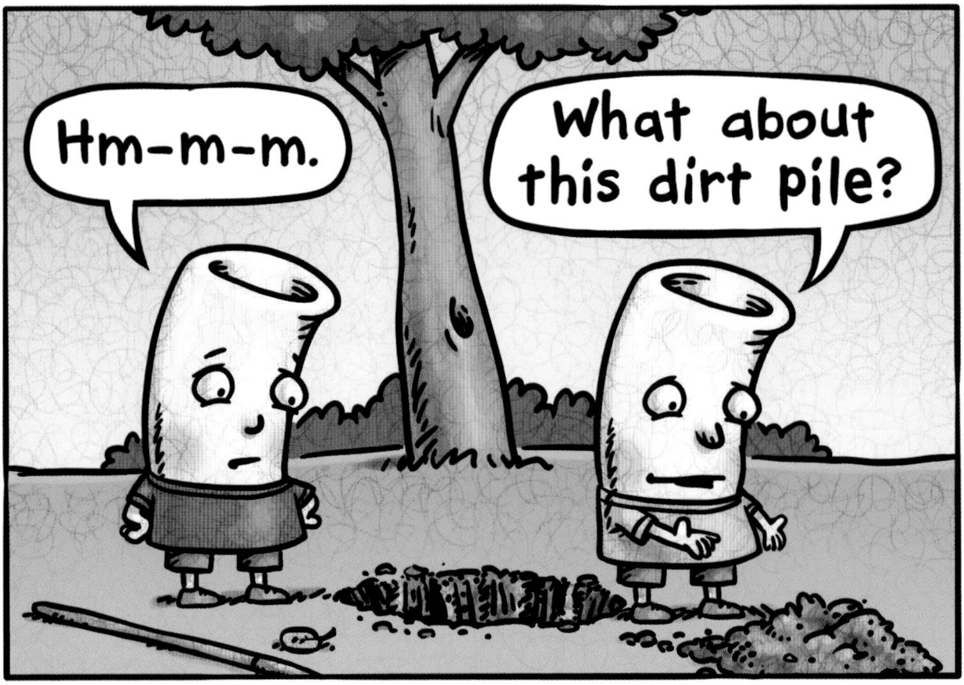
Hm-m-m.
What about this dirt pile?

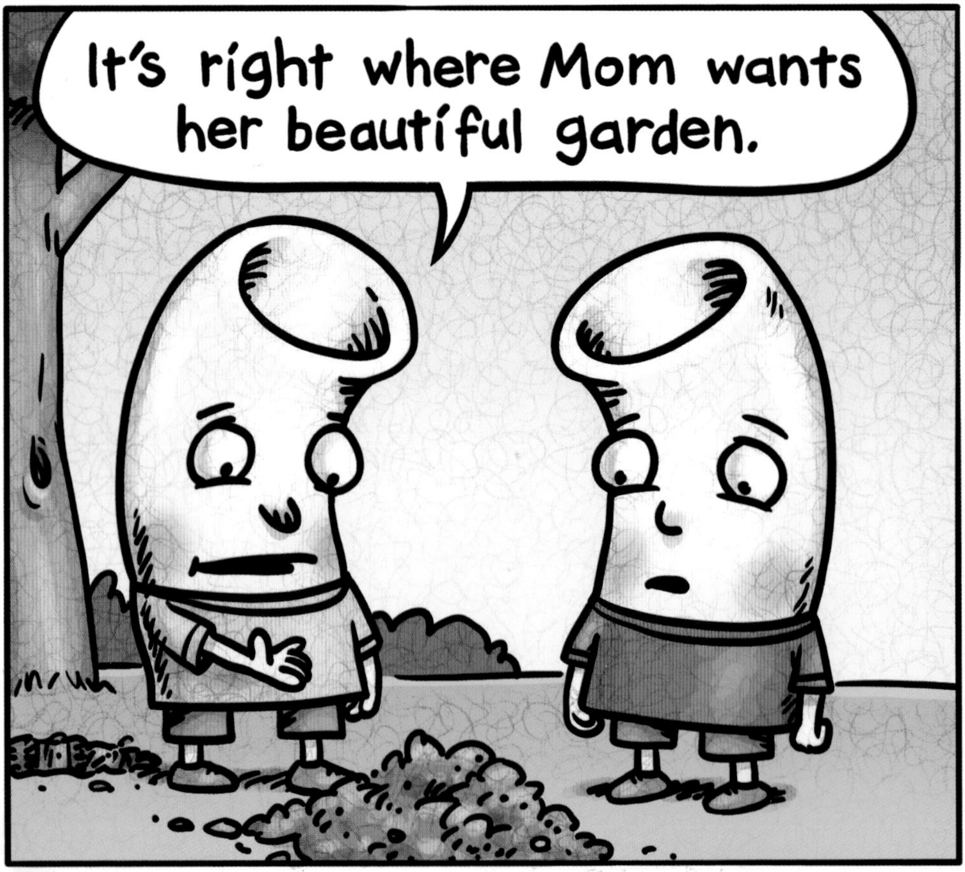
It's right where Mom wants her beautiful garden.

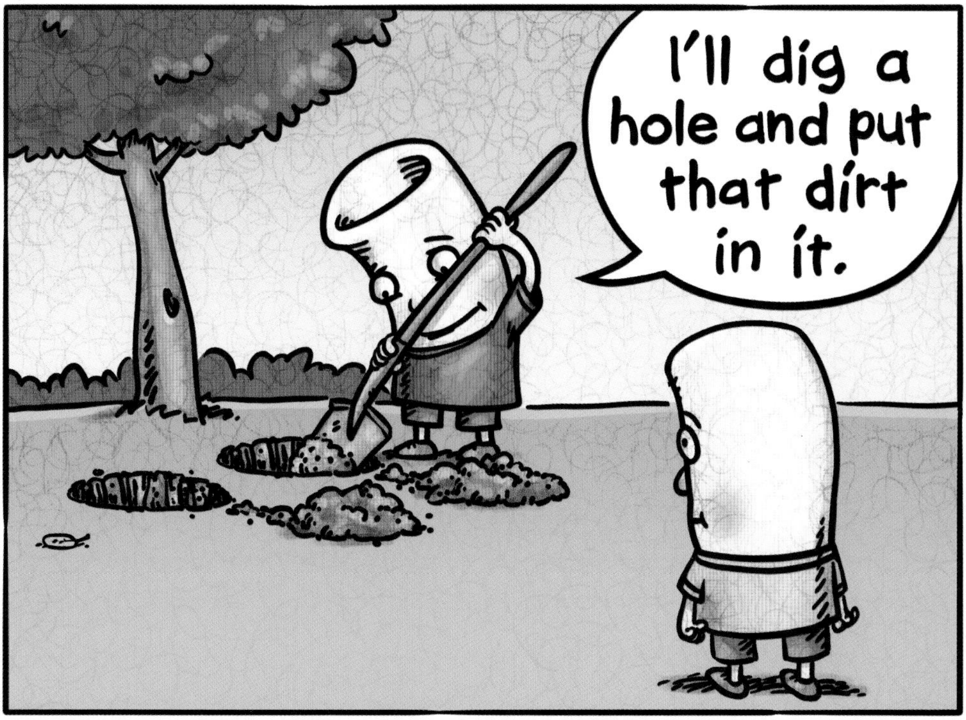
I'll dig a hole and put that dirt in it.

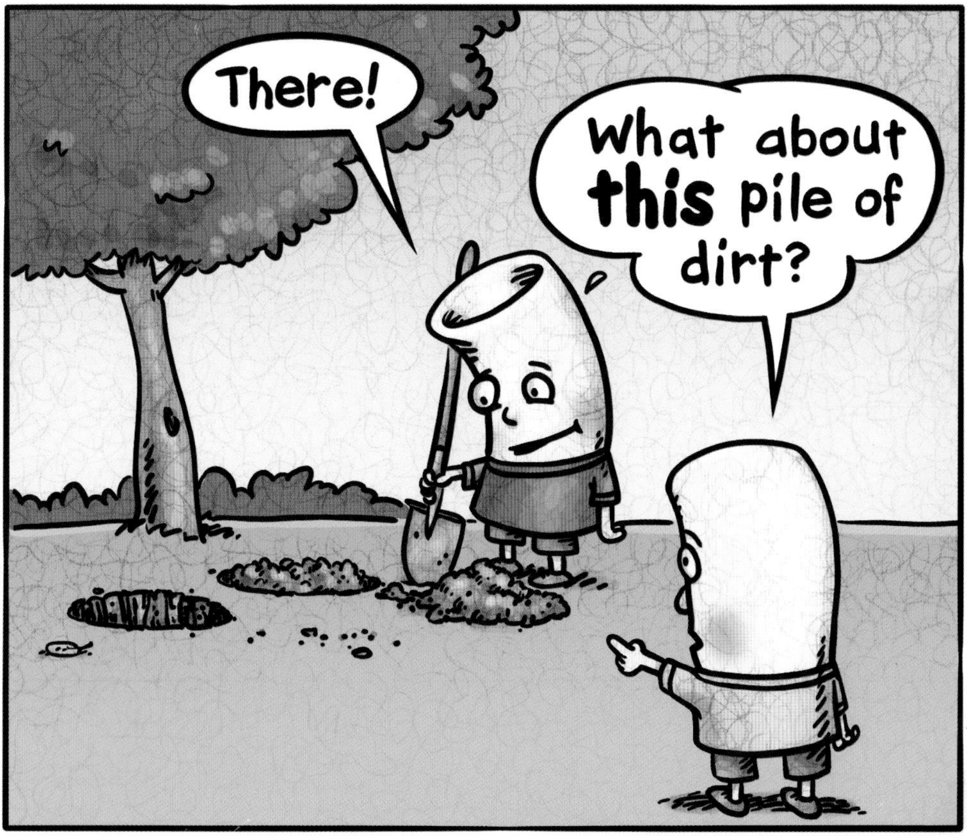
There!
What about **this** pile of dirt?

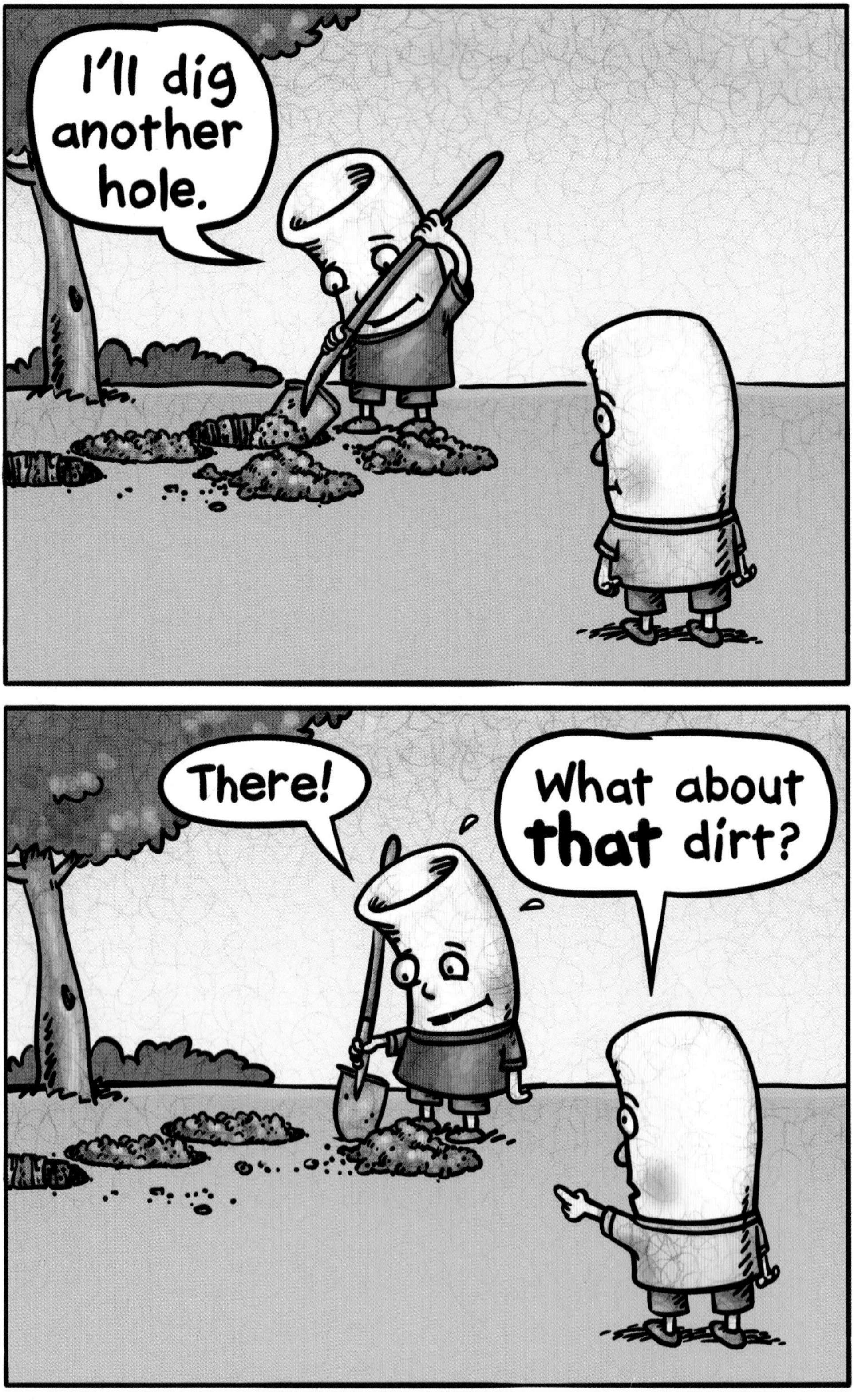
I'll dig another hole.
There!
What about **that** dirt?

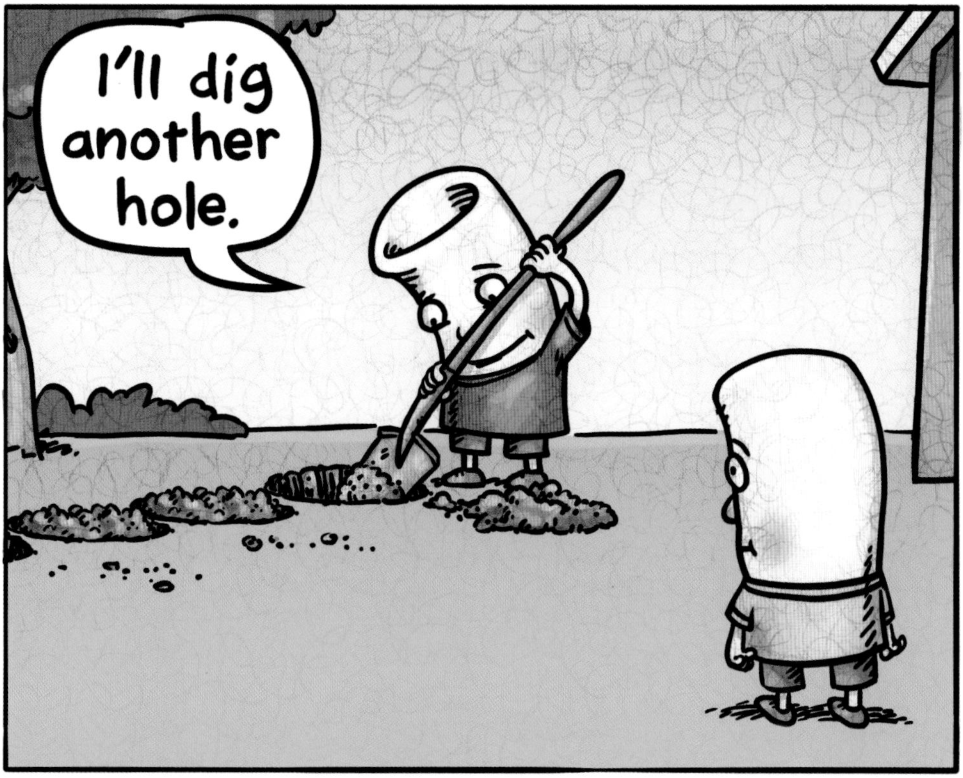
I'll dig another hole.

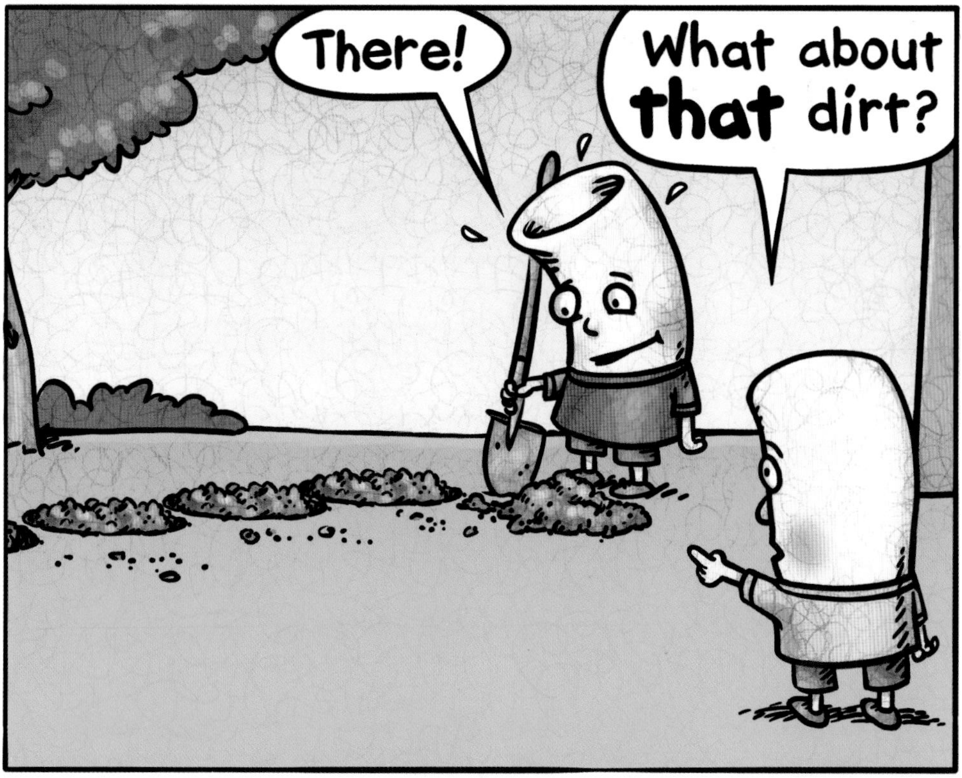
There!
What about **that** dirt?

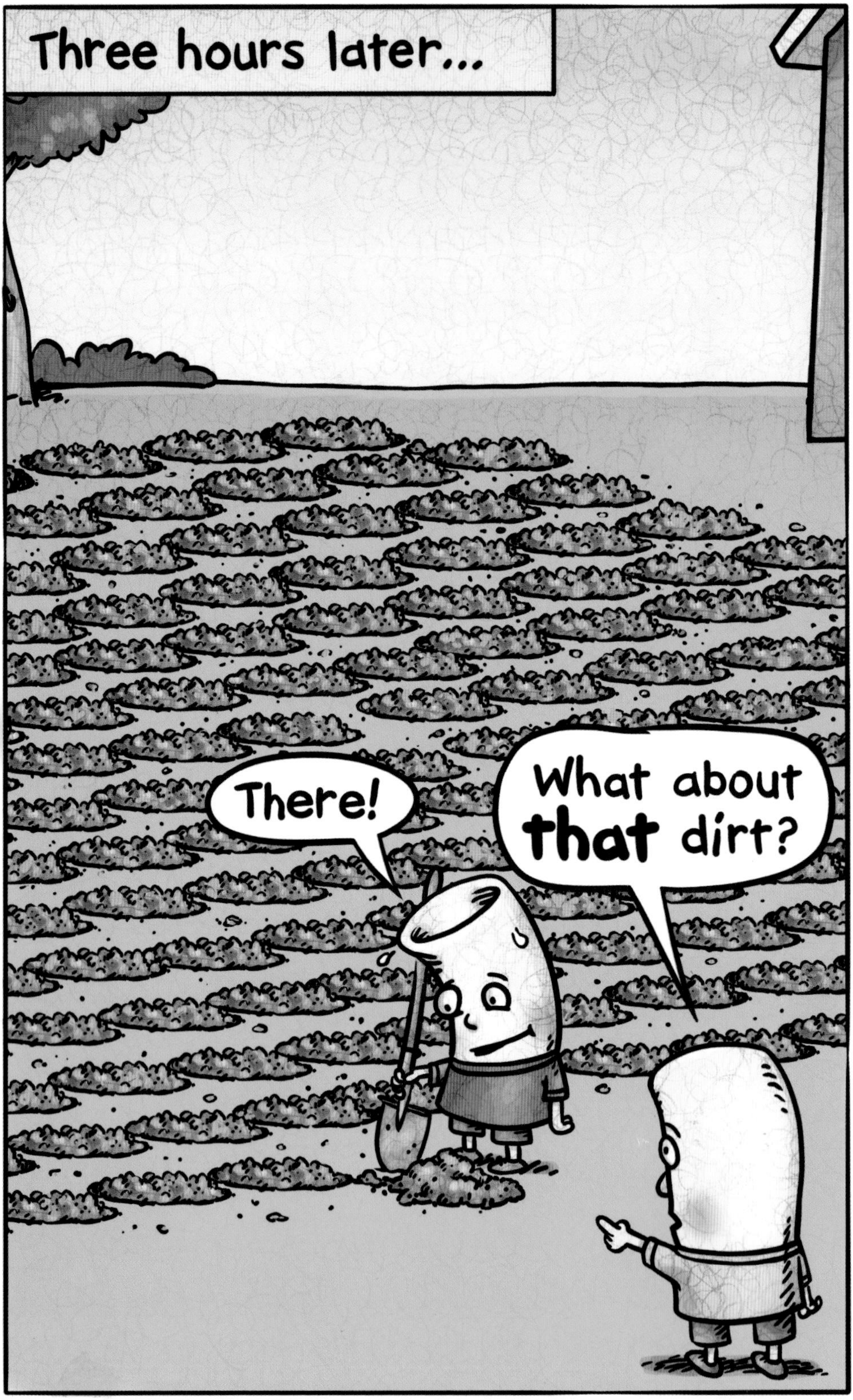
Three hours later...
There!
What about **that** dirt?

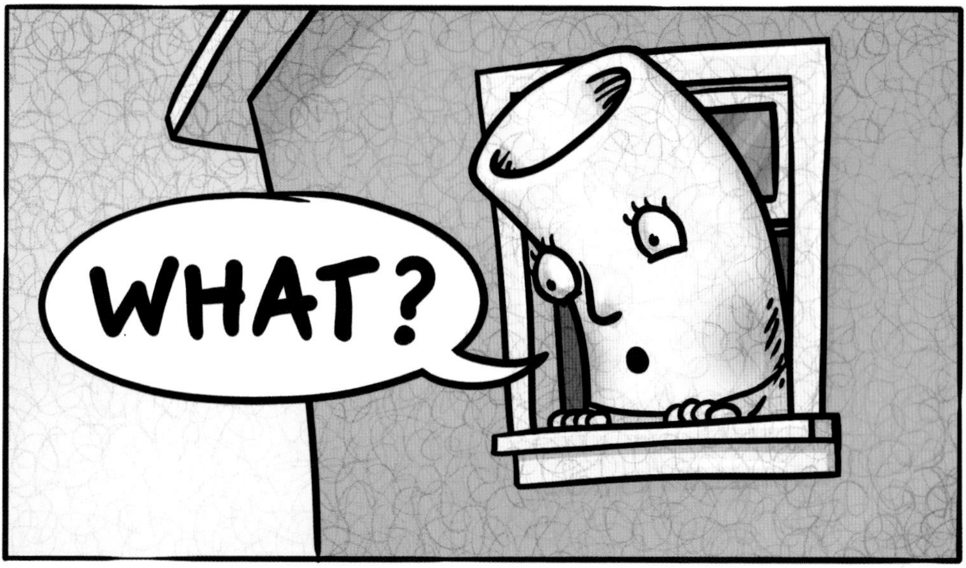
WHAT?

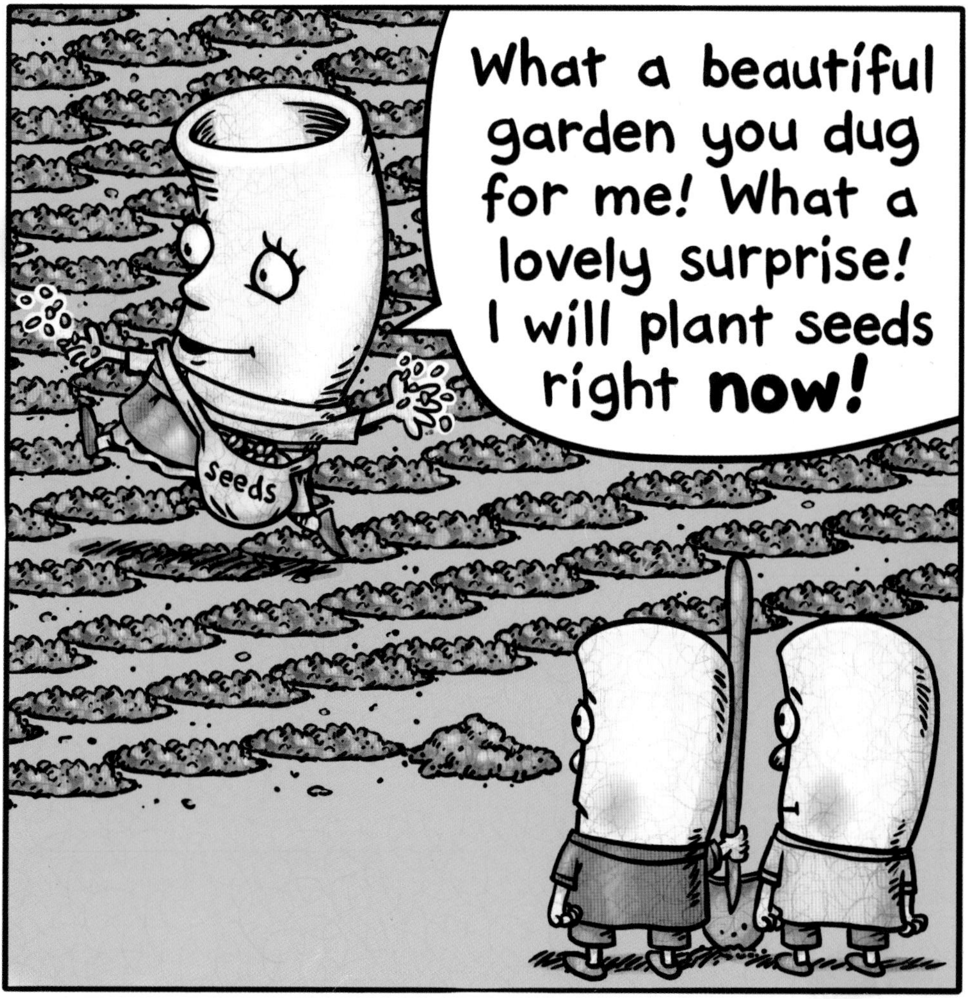
seeds
What a beautiful garden you dug for me! What a lovely surprise! I will plant seeds right **now!**

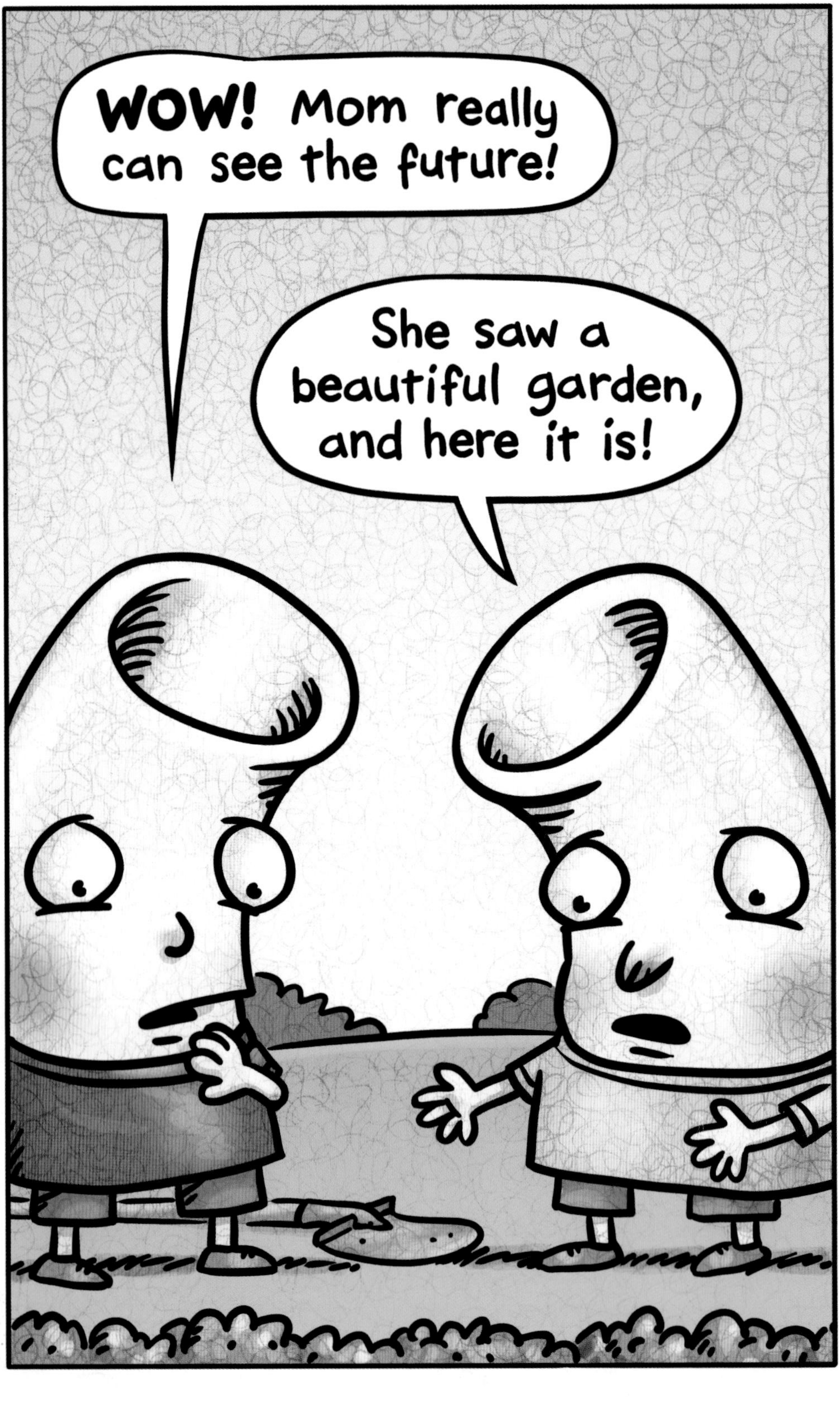
WOW! Mom really can see the future!
She saw a beautiful garden, and here it is!

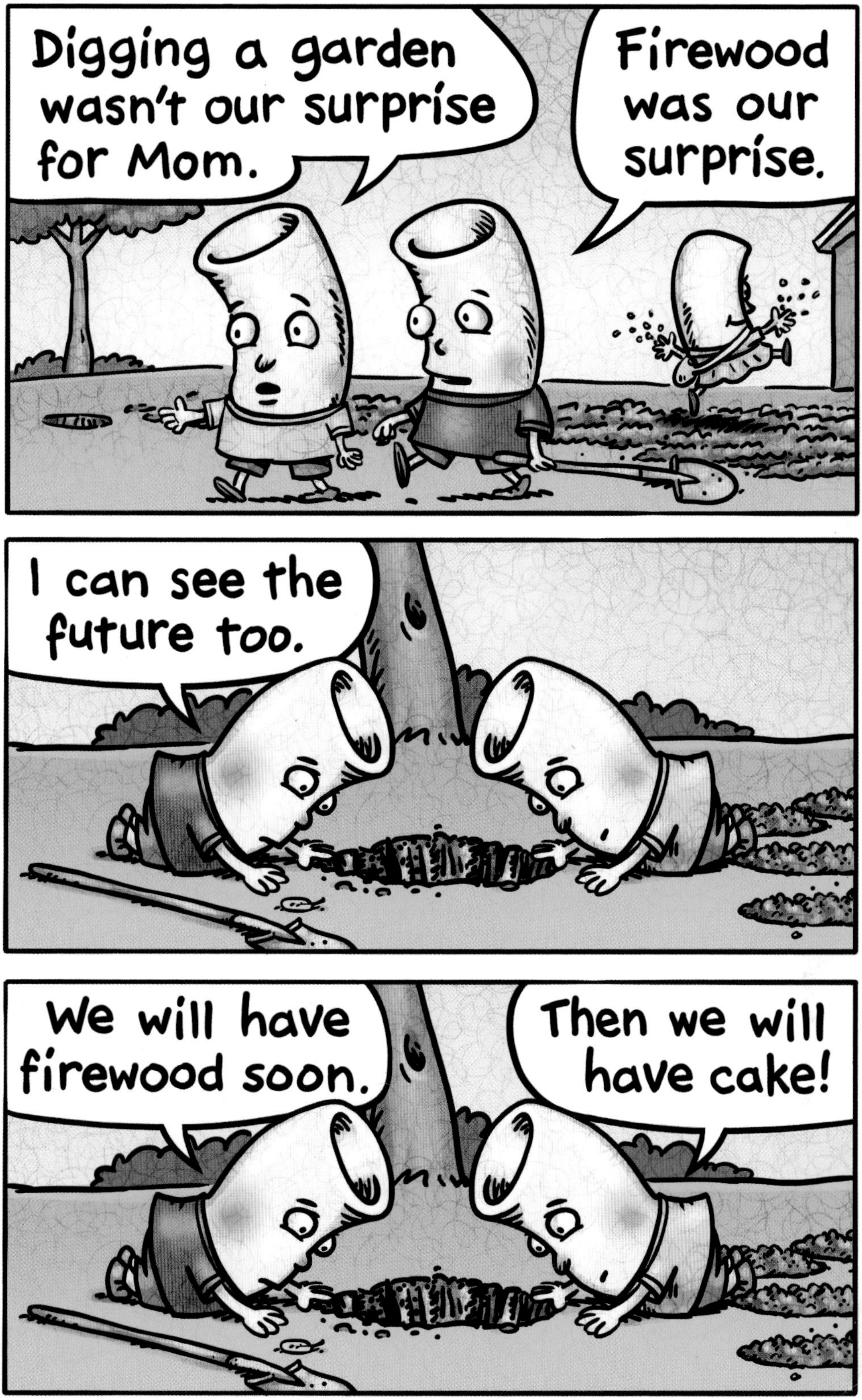
Digging a garden wasn't our surprise for Mom.
Firewood was our surprise.
I can see the future too.
We will have firewood soon.
Then we will have cake!

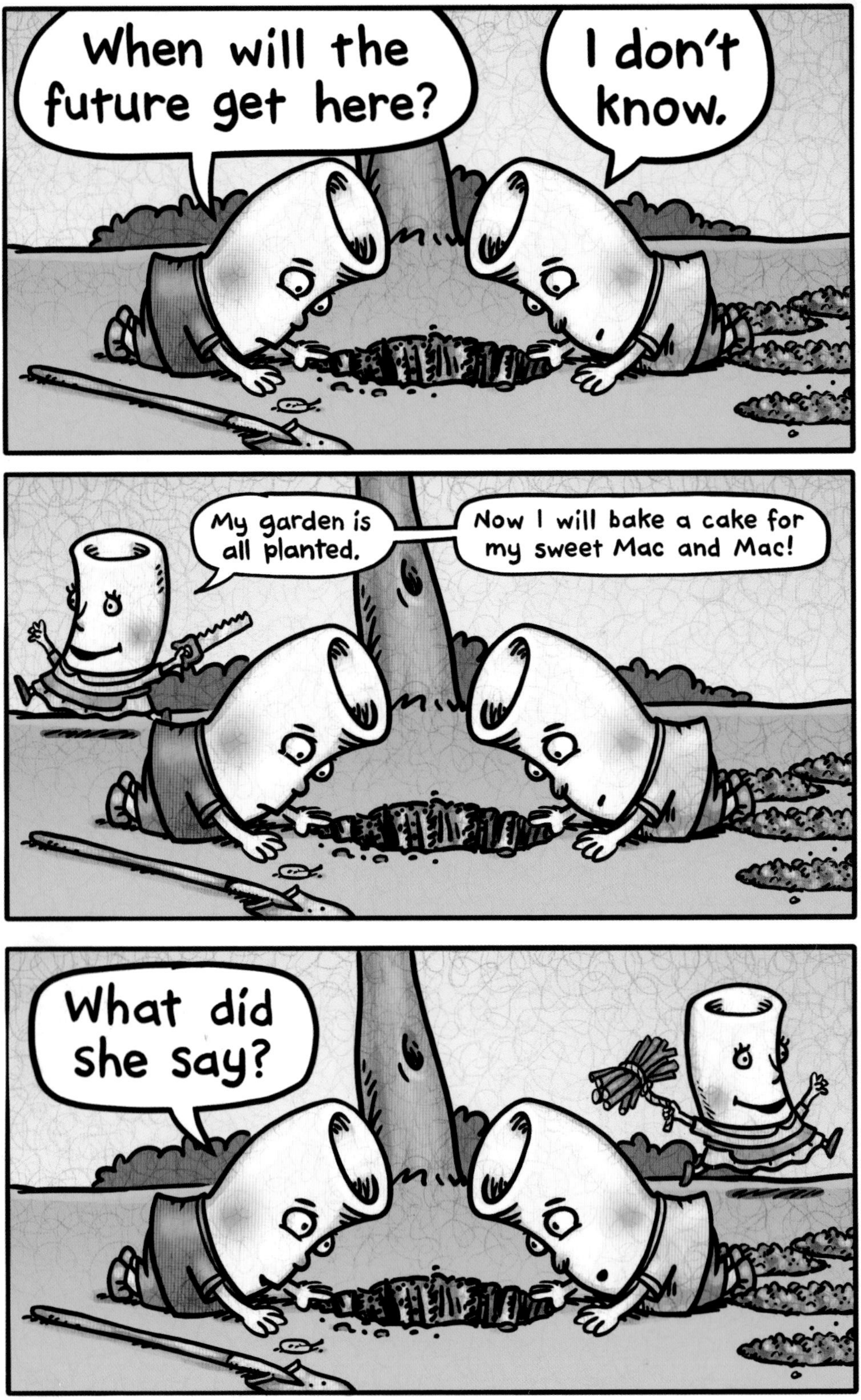
When will the future get here?
I don't know.
My garden is all planted.
Now I will bake a cake for my sweet Mac and Mac!
What did she say?

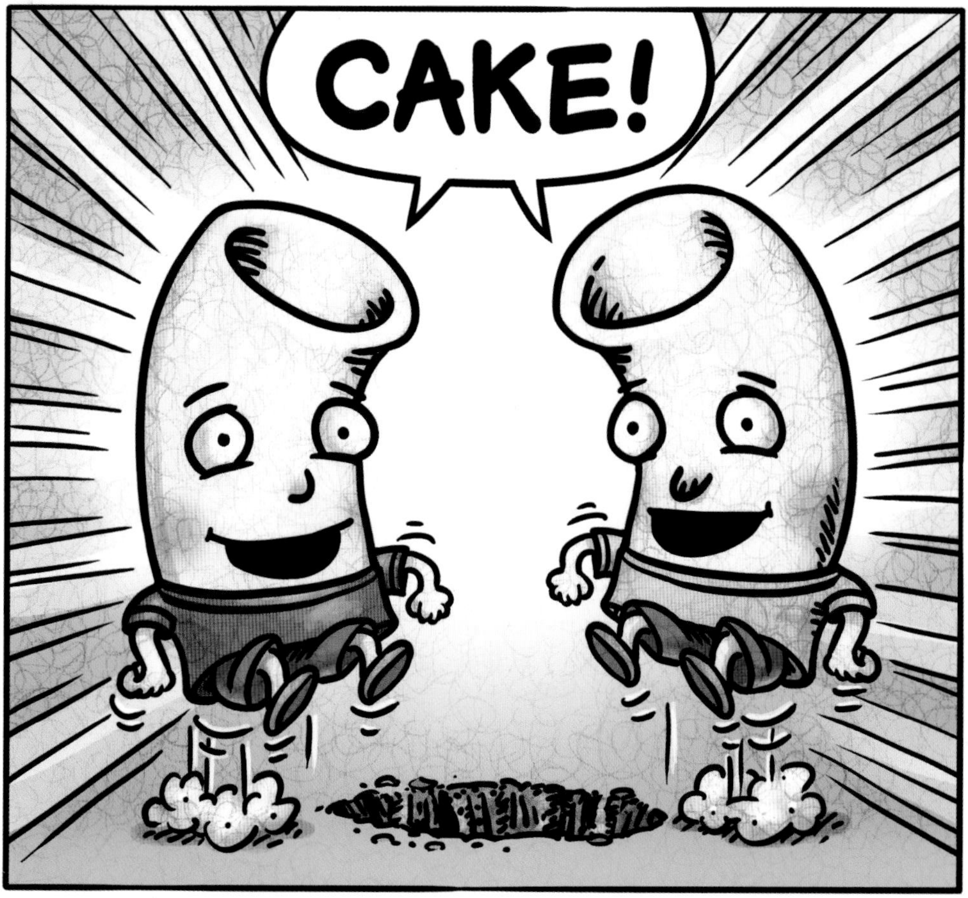
CAKE!

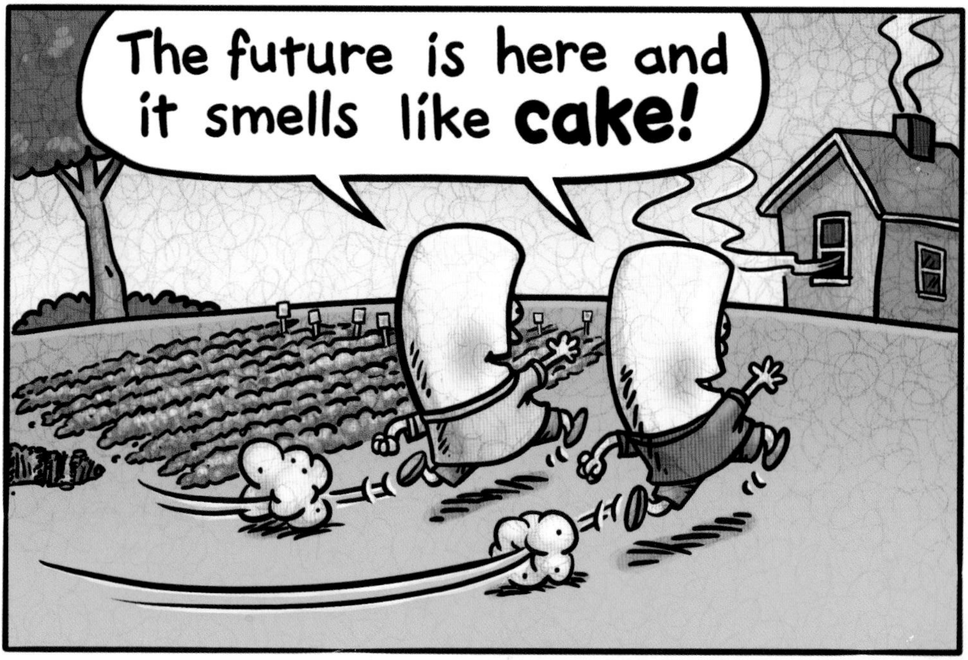
The future is here and it smells like cake!

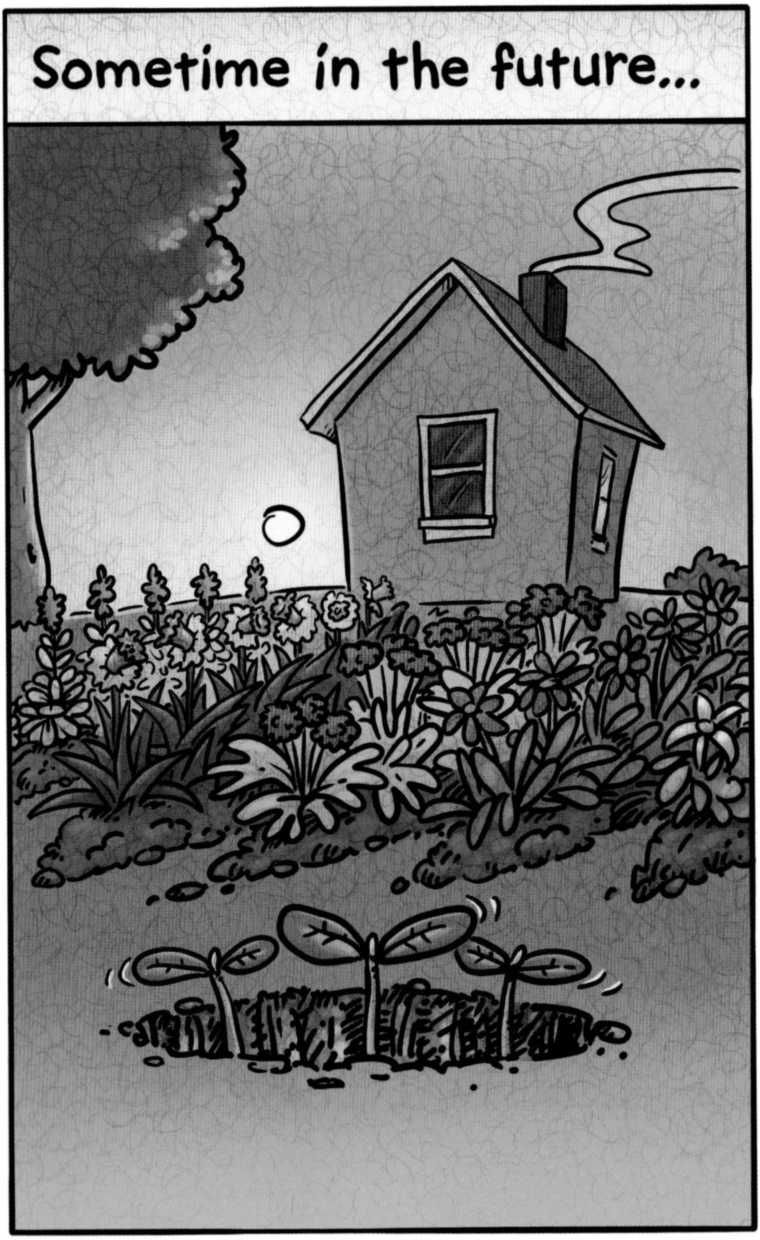
Sometime in the future...

Authors' Notes

Story Sources for *Noodleheads See the Future*

Everyone has done something foolish at one time or another. As a result, tales of fools, also called "noodles" or "noodleheads," have been told for as long as people have told stories. In 1888, W. A. Clouston wrote a scholarly book called *The Book of Noodles* in which he describes numerous stories that had been told for hundreds of years, and quite a few dating back over two millennia. We have used these old stories as inspiration for Mac and Mac's adventures. People around the world tell similar stories about their particular fools, such as Giufà in Italy, Nasreddin Hodja in Turkey, Juan Bobo in Puerto Rico, and Jack in England. The expression "Fortune, that favors fools" is apt, for, in spite of their foolishness, things usually turn out fine in the end for the fool. Perhaps this is because they are generally kind and well-meaning. Noodlehead stories help children to understand humor and logical thinking; kids quickly see that noodleheads are totally illogical—usually to an absurd extent.

The motifs to which we refer in the information that follows are from *The Storyteller's Sourcebook: A Subject, Title, and Motif Index to Folklore Collections for Children* by Margaret Read MacDonald, first edition (Detroit: Gale, 1982) and second edition (Detroit: Gale, 2001). Tale types are from *The Types of the Folktale* by Antti Aarne and Stith Thompson (Helsinki: Folklore Fellows Communication, 1961) and *A Guide to Folktales in the English Language* by D. L. Ashliman (NY: Greenwood, 1987).

—Getting Firewood—

The inspiration for several of the events in this story can be found in "Dead or Alive," a Uruguayan folktale in *Noodlehead Stories: World Tales Kids Can Read and Tell* by Martha Hamilton and Mitch Weiss (Atlanta: August House Publishers, 2001). The motif in this chapter is J2133.4, *Numskull cuts off tree limb on which he is sitting.* In the many world tales with this motif, someone comes along and warns the fool that he will fall. When this inevitably happens, the fool, rather than thinking that the person was sharing commonsense advice, comes to the conclusion that the person can predict the future.

— The Talking Dead —

The fool searches out the "fortune-teller" to find out when he will die and is given a flippant answer—which he believes, regardless of evidence to the contrary. He lies down and closes his eyes. In many versions, he realizes he is not dead when he gets hungry. There is also a common motif of him speaking up to settle an argument about which way to go while he is being carried to the graveyard. The tale type for this chapter is 1313A, *Prediction of death taken seriously.* Motifs include J2311.1, *Numskull is told he will die when . . . ,* and J2311.4, *The dead man speaks up.* The inspiration for acorns as "firewood seeds" was J1770, *Objects with mistaken identity.* This often involves someone tricking a fool into believing that, for example, a pumpkin is a "horse egg." See Cynthia DeFelice's *Mule Eggs* (New York: Orchard Books, 1994) or "The Donkey Egg" in *Noodlehead Stories*, cited above. In this chapter, Meatball's trick has some truth because acorns do turn into trees and eventually could become firewood. Of course, it doesn't simply happen with a "POOF!" Noodlehead stories make children aware of the problems that can be caused by being gullible.

— Seeing the Future —

Another common noodlehead motif is J1934, *A hole to throw the earth in.* In a version from Germany, some townsfolk dig a well and don't know what to do with the dirt, so they decide to dig a second hole to put it in. When one person points out that they will need a place to put the dirt from the second hole, the mayor (people in power are often noodleheads in the old stories) suggests that they just dig the second hole big enough to hold the dirt from both holes. See *Folktales of Germany* by Kurt Ranke (Chicago: University of Chicago Press, 1966).